HEART OF THE ROCKIES

QUEEN OF THE ROCKIES — BOOK 3

ANGELA BREIDENBACH

© 2016, 2019, 2021 by Angela E Breidenbach, LLC
ISBN (ebook) 978-0-9827172-9-5
ISBN (Pbk) 978-0-9980847-0-1
ISBN (Large Print) 978-1-957132-00-6
Published by Gems Books, an imprint of Gems of Wisdom
Contact for questions and permissions: angela@angelabreidenbach.com
Breidenbach, Angela
Heart of the Rockies/Angela E. Breidenbach, LLC
1. Fiction 2. Romance—Fiction 3. Historical—Fiction
This book is a work of fiction set in a real location. Any reference to historical figures, places, or events, whether fictional or actual, is a fictional representation.
Biblical verses used in this work of fiction are taken from the (RV) Revised Version 1885 and are Public Domain.
Published in Missoula, MT

Thank you, Mor-Mor (Grandma — Mother's Mother in Swedish), for showing me that synchronized swimming could be an amazing hobby at any age. You inspired me to keep exploring life and finding joy in the beauty of dancing in the water.

INTRODUCTION

This story, the third in the Queen of the Rockies series, celebrates a glorious time in the 1890s as well as women's rights and the pioneers that paved the roads for us. In Charles A. Broadwater's case, he literally created the transportation network starting in 1862, with goods serving miners and military by wagons. Then, he helped build the railroads in Montana, too.

It's an honor to feature this great man who spent thirty years building an infrastructure, banking, and tourism to help us become the state we are today and still be known as a kind and gracious person. How blessed we are, others went before us. When the colonel passed, over 5,000 people came to pay their respects from all over the state—a significant percentage of the population of Montana at the time. Would that my life could have such an impact!

Though it's unknown to me whether the Broadwater Natatorium had any swimming teams or instruction, because of the era I'm assuming/creating them for the purpose of story. The first women's competitions began in

Europe in 1890-91. The first synchronized swimming teams were called ornamental or scientific (lifesaving techniques). They used more floating routines than diving, flips, or intense underwater tricks that we see today. Those additions came a few years later as my favorite sport developed into a beautiful water ballet that my grandmother performed as a hobby. Then I did, too. The athleticism is difficult and incredible!

The Hotel Broadwater and Natatorium were real places. But they've been relegated to the mists of time, much like Camelot, becoming a bit larger than life in Montana history. But that blend of myth and mystery are well deserved.

Charles A. Broadwater is a major figure in Montana history. His family and his incredible business successes are also real. But again, for the sake of story, I've taken literary license in creating swimming teams his daughter might participate in (Wilder's skill-level in the water, any or none, is unknown to me) and any dialogue is my fictional invention. I've tried to remain true to historical facts about the life and death of this beloved Montanan and his creation, the Hotel Broadwater and Natatorium. If you'd like more information on it, be sure to read the Travel Tips at the back of this book. I'll note a few research aids used to prepare for this fun journey back in time. Please grant me grace where fiction takes over from fact in creating this story for you. Put yourself in that space and time. See the era, society, and people through the lens of history and not the modern way of life.

Thank you for going on the journey with me,
Angela Breidenbach

CHAPTER 1

Late winter, 1892, Helena, MT

Delphina O'Connor ran to the edge of the plunge. "Kick up!" Was that Mr. Broadwater's daughter in the deep end? Delphina strained to see in the darker waters of the deep end. The electric lamplight didn't quite reach far enough to tell who fell in, but she wasn't succeeding in getting out! The young girl thrashed against the heavy woolen skirt of her swim costume. She couldn't keep her head above the hot springs pumped into the monstrous indoor pool.

Grabbing the pole hook from the wall, Delphina stretched out as far as she could. But soon the youngster would no longer break the surface to see the lifesaver. "Calm down, grab on!"

Panicking, she took in more water than air. Terror overtook the waterlogged child as she thrashed and knocked the pole away. Delphina couldn't get hold of the swim outfit either. It slipped off the hook each time the girl twisted. The girl's hands couldn't reach the surface in the twelve-foot depths, and she was fatiguing fast.

Bubbles.

Knowing how to swim wouldn't help when both woolen skirts would drag them down. But she had to try. "Help! I need help!" A quick glance around proved no one else had entered the natatorium yet. Did no one hear her scream?

She threw the pole hook on the deck, took a deep breath, and jumped. Warm water sucked her under as she swam hard. She kept her eyes on the dark, descending figure as the girl went limp. Kicking her swimming slippers as hard as she could, Delphina managed to get a hand on the girl's billowing sleeve and yanked at the material. But she couldn't budge the weight of sopping wool more than a smidgeon. The girl was closer to Delphina's size than she'd realized. Both costumes swirled around them like the jellyfish in an inky dark ocean.

She pointed her shoulders at the plunge wall and kicked harder, with every ounce of effort in her being, until her legs burned and her arms felt numb. For a moment, the surface tickled at her face, but Delphina couldn't stretch above it to catch the air she needed to propel them both to safety and gulped half water with the oxygen. Delphina willed her body, and the one she towed upward. Instead of surfacing for air, the two sank further toward the bottom. The skylights retreating into pinpoints of blurred light. Burning lungs, a screaming cough clawing at her throat, Delphina refused to let go of the adolescent.

Muscular arms closed around her torso from behind and thrust her toward the surface. Still, she wouldn't release the ruffle her fingers clutched. Up. Up. More arms grabbed at hers and fought to pry the limp girl away as liquid gave way to air.

Delphina sucked in half a stomach full of water as she gasped for life a moment too soon. Then she choked, coughed, and heaved out what she'd taken in. Nose burning, ragged gasps, and more coughing racked her ribs until she fell exhausted on the pool deck, trembling from the exertion. A shadow fell on her face, blocking the natural light from the natatorium's windows high above.

A man's voice directed towards the skirmish further down the planked deck. "Arms above her head. Press her stomach." He called orders to others even as the man's big hands thrust Delphina's arms above her head. "Turn her over and get the water out of her." He flipped Delphina like a rag doll and spanned her back with one hand. He waited for a breath, then flapjacked her back and watched her face for signs of life. Seeming satisfied, he stood and turned to supervise the boys following his lifesaving orders.

The shadow man moved away, leaving Delphina sprawling on the pool deck in the least ladylike manner, skirts as scattered as driftwood. Lifting to her elbows, Delphina watched Wilder spew more water than a body should be able to hold. But she survived! Delphina lay back and thanked God. She took a deep breath, grateful for the other rescuers and the sweet feeling of dry air moving in and out of her chest.

Her rescuer returned. "What do you think you two were doing swimming in the deep end in those costumes?"

She'd feel much more comfortable if the man's features were visible. After all, he'd had his hands all over her. But the light pouring in from the windows above produced backlighting, drowning his face in shadows. "What?" Delphina's head throbbed, and her ears needed unclogging.

He fired off another question like dynamite near the mines. "Don't you know better?"

She squeezed her burning eyes and blinked a few times, trying to distinguish more about the man towering above than the outline of his legs askew, fists jammed on hips. His darker hair dripped down on her like rain spattering saturated ground. As her vision adjusted to the ethereal illusions of color in geometric patterns created by the immense stain glass windows, electric lamps, and arced cathedral ceilings inside the natatorium, his angry eyes crackled like lightning over the Montana mountains.

"What?" She shook her head and blinked hard as she threw the heavy braid behind her shoulder. The length and weight of the sopping plait so great it slapped the wooden floor like a mop.

"I said," he paused, creating a stern effect, "you obviously need to return to your governesses. The two of you almost drowned."

Governesses? "I don't need a governess. I am—"

"If you can't avoid danger by yourself, then you must be under the care of an adult."

Enough. Only her first day in position and already a near drowning incident. Delphina shoved to her shaking knees and then to standing. The heavy skirts of the swimming costume threatened to drag her right back down. Planting her hands on her hips as he'd done, she snapped back, "I am an adult, sir, and I'll have you know—"

"Adults don't behave irresponsibly." He glared at her.

She wanted to scream at this insulting stranger. Then she remembered he'd saved not only her life, but also

Wilder's. The girl who was in her care and the daughter of her new employer. She closed her eyes and deliberately lowered her hands to her sides with a long, long inhale and exhale. "First, let me say thank you."

"Don't. Just be more careful." He called to the dozen or so gathered around them. "Boys, let's get all this gear cleaned up and ready for laps."

She tightened her lips against her teeth. Teeth that wanted to bite all of a sudden at his imperial tone. "Sir, I was not irresponsible. I was, in fact, trying to save Miss Broadwater."

His head jerked back in surprise. For a moment, his handsome face registered astonishment… and then he chuckled. The chuckle rippled into an all-out laugh, thundering as it echoed in the cavernous building.

Delphina's face rushed with warmth. "That's quite enough, sir. You may have saved our lives." She looked around at the other dripping young men gathered around them. "But you have no right to insult either one of us. Exactly who are you anyway?"

"Hugh Thomas, the swimming instructor, luckily for you. And you would be?"

Her eyes narrowed. "Ah, the swimming instructor for the men." What a chauvinist! "I would be the scientific and ornamental swimming instructress for the women."

The man's eyebrows lifted. "The what?" He jolted with a laugh and then sobered when he took a look at the group helping Wilder Broadwater. He shook his head, flinging water droplets around them. "Then I'll suggest you be replaced immediately."

She gasped. Unfortunately, as she did, the water still streaming from her hair sucked into her windpipe.

Coughing the water out of her lungs doubled Delphina over and delayed the dramatic delivery she'd planned.

She pointed a finger at him until she rose to standing. To her surprise, he waited. "You'll do no such thing!" Her words would be so much more convincing if she didn't cough through the water streaming down her face from the mass of tangled hair.

"Just get it all out." He landed several smart slaps on her back, causing more hacking than necessary, in Delphina's opinion. "You'll feel much better."

"You—" She held up a hand, signaling for him to stop and jammed the other against the unexpected sharp stitch in her side. "Don't touch me!" Her words came out more like a hoarse tom cat.

He walked away. "Miss Broadwater, let's get you to a chair." As he gently sat the teary girl on a chair, one of the many young men grabbed and deposited nearby. "Towels? Let's get some towels around these girls."

Delphina's eyes widened. He could be kind to Antoinette Wilder Broadwater, but not to the woman who tried to save her life? What an impolite heathen! Then the warmth of a towel wrapped around Delphina, and a gangly boy propelled her to another chair near Wilder's.

She looked up and nodded her appreciation. "Thank you."

He answered with a kind voice, "My pleasure, miss."

Hugh's directions scrambled the group into action as they cleaned the deck of lifesaving equipment. "Frankie, throw on a dry robe and fetch Miss Broadwater's parents. They'll want to know immediately."

"Yes, sir, Mr. Thomas." The boy that'd been caring for Delphina bobbed his head and took off to his errand.

What was he, all of fourteen? Still, he had more manners than his uncouth instructor. But Wilder had been given into her care this afternoon. "I'll get your mother, Wilder." Delphina rose, but the low chair caught at her swimming costume. She fell forward, catching herself on the heels of her hands, preventing her face from smacking into the wood deck, but splayed on the ground in a most unladylike fashion—again.

"Miss O'Connor!" Wilder called. "Are you all right?"

The next second, strong hands clasped around her waist and hauled her up to her feet like a pile of laundry. "Go on, Frankie. I have this under control."

Delphina closed her eyes to stop the tears of both pain and embarrassment, as she pressed hot, stinging hands against the cooler folds of the wet swim skirt. "Thank you," she swallowed her pride. "Thank you, again." Delphina could not bring herself to offer even a polite smile.

He stood too close, hands still on her waist, and leaned down to her ear so only she could hear him. "I fear dance instructor is not a good idea either." His chuckle tickled the skin behind her ear.

Why did his voice sing in her veins?

THE GIRL'S eyes sparked a deep amber fire. She shook free of his sturdy hands. "Unbelievable!" She pushed him away. "You have no idea who I am or what I'm capable of and yet you presume to judge my abilities!"

He wanted to laugh at the girl smoothing the mass of sopping hair out of her eyes, but the seriousness of lives nearly lost subdued Hugh. "What I know is you're too young and inexperienced for this position."

Wilder chose this moment to pipe up. "Oh, Miss O'Connor's not too young. She's a spinster."

At the child's unfiltered input, the swim instructress nearly turned purple under the tangled mass of hair the color of evergreen bark after a downpour on a spring day. Hugh couldn't help himself. He tossed off a grin that broke into a rumbling laugh. "I see."

"Wilder!" Miss O'Connor spun to chastise the owner's daughter. Then she obviously grappled for words before giving up and turning back on him. "I'll have you know, sir, that I have a teaching degree from Vassar and that I focused on the science of health—and that includes an excellent knowledge of swimming and lifesaving."

"Then you of all people should know better than to swim with all," he gestured at the voluminous swimwear, "that on in the deep end of a pool."

"I did not—"

"Wilder, oh Wilder," Mrs. Broadwater swept into the natatorium. "Dear heart, please tell me you're all right." She clasped the wet girl tightly to her bosom, not caring about her clothing.

"I believe she'll be fine, ma'am."

"Is that the case, Miss O'Connor?"

"I'm sorry, Mrs. Broadwater, I haven't been able to check Wilder myself. I've been," she tipped her head toward Hugh, "detained for questioning."

"Wilder, what happened?" Mrs. Broadwater pulled her daughter's chin up with her hand and scrutinized her.

"Mama, I ran out to place a candy order for after swimming. You know how hungry I get after being in the water." She hung her head. "But I slipped in when I went around that corner." She pointed to where the railing stopped. Her shoulders slumped as her mother's eyes narrowed. "Miss O'Connor jumped in after me. Then all these boys saved us both."

"Candy." Hugh choked back a growl. "You both almost drowned for a candy?"

Wilder's eyes brimmed. "I didn't mean to do that." Puppy dog eyes plead up at her parents as Mr. Broadwater joined the crowd.

"Ah, but you did, young lady." Her father's stern voice caused a cavalcade of tears. He peered through round spectacles at his pocket watch. "The counter isn't open for another thirty minutes. What possessed you to race in so early?"

She mumbled, "I didn't think Mama would let me have any." Tears streaked down her cheeks.

Miss O'Connor popped into the momentary lull. "Wilder, this is exactly why the rules for not running on the deck are there. With your parents as the owners, it's even more important for you to set the example for the other girls and boys who come to take a plunge." Then she turned to the Broadwaters. "Would you consider sitting your daughter out for the next class as a discipline? She should have to dress out and sit on the side so she can still learn from the instruction."

Evidently, Miss O'Connor told the truth. But was she their governess or his employee?

"No, Papa! That's not fair!"

"I think that's not fair either, my girl." He agreed.

"But sir—" Miss O'Connor started.

He held up a hand. "I didn't build this entire resort just to have my only daughter misuse it. Nor did I build this natatorium to lose her." Charles Broadwater pursed his lips as everyone waited for his decision. "Wilder will sit out, as you've suggested. In addition, the temptation that caused the poor behavior is also removed." He directed his attention to the young girl. "You've also lost your purchasing privileges at the shop yonder for the classes Miss O'Connor chooses to sit you out."

"Papa, that's really not fair!" She whined.

"I will notify the staff. Should Miss O'Connor need to make this decision again, the two parts will make the whole."

"But—"

"Evidently I need to add more discipline before you learn a lesson?"

She hung her head, light hair and a limp blue ribbon drooped over her shoulders in a stringy mass. Poor girl resembled more of a cocker spaniel at the moment. "No, sir."

Hugh folded his arms. He rather liked his employer's way of thinking and handling of his daughter. The colonel hadn't once raised his voice. "Sir, if I may, the women cannot survive in the deep end. Twelve feet is not safe for a lady, even one who thinks she can swim." Then he pointedly glanced in Miss O'Connor's direction. "Might I suggest a cord across the pool at the four-foot mark? I don't believe the ladies should venture deeper than four feet. The risk, as we've seen, is too great."

"Just one minute. There's no need to limit the ladies to the shallow end." Miss O'Connor leapt to the defense of womankind everywhere. "This was an unusual circumstance. In fact, I've been able to swim—"

"I did not see proof of that today, Miss O'Connor." He stepped closer. "In fact, I saw exactly the opposite as I saved your life."

Everyone craned to catch up with the last banter, bebopping back and forth between them like birdies on the badminton court. "Indeed, you did not, sir!" As her hair dried, it unraveled into frizzy ropes that hung like Rapunzel's locks. Did she know how comical she appeared? "What you saw were two bodies fighting heavy woolens in the water. You did not see my lack of ability to swim. You couldn't have—"

"You're making the point, Miss O'Connor. I pulled you

both up with great effort and then all these boys assisted getting you and Wilder on the deck."

"Why was that, Mr. Swim Instructor? Were we too heavy for you to get out of the water yourself?"

Mr. Swim Instructor.

"I do believe you've made my point."

He meant to answer. He opened his mouth, about to, and then Hugh realized she was right. All five foot two of her and he'd needed help with the weight of those skirts.

Colonel Broadwater took the reins of the conversation. "What I'm hearing is that my daughter nearly drowned because of her swim costume and that her teacher, and a very fit man, both had trouble because of these contraptions you ladies wear. Is that what you're telling me?"

Both instructors answered at once, "Yes." Their eyes were drawn to one another. Hugh's were then drawn down the drenched lady in front of him. He couldn't really tell much of any detail under all that droopy black fabric. How many sheep were shorn for that outfit? Was there a woman under there? But something about the flaring fire in her eyes made him swallow. Hard.

"Besides my daughter's safety, these swimming costumes are putting any lady that enjoys the natatorium at risk. Is that what you're telling me?"

Miss O'Connor nodded vigorously at his words while Hugh contemplated the unknown world of women's fashion. If that's what they wore, that's what they wore. "Sir, this is why we need to create some sort of warning mark. The ladies shouldn't go beyond for their own safety."

She twitched as if struck. "No, that is not what we need."

Miss O'Connor's inability to allow the men to protect

her scorched his nerves. "If not that, then I can see the need to post extra lifeguards at all times."

"Are you completely out of your mind? Women are not cattle to be guarded from rustlers."

"Can you be any less practical?"

"My goodness, but your creativity astounds me." Miss O'Connor stepped around him as if he was inconsequential, and her tone stung with a reprimand. How did he think she was a child? "Truly, don't you think there's another way?"

Then she turned her back on him. Unthinkable for a civilized lady toward her betters. Did she just accuse him of being an imbecile? "Excuse me." Irritation seethed between his teeth.

As she peeked over her shoulder, a hint of a smile tipped the corner of her mouth. "Of course." She blinked innocently as if she meant it, and then addressed Charles Broadwater. "I think the best opportunity we have for the safety of women from here on out would be to adopt the new swimming costumes European women are wearing. That does away with all this excess fabric dragging a person under."

Mrs. Broadwater gasped. "But modesty, Charles, we must protect the modesty of our patrons."

"I wore a much less bulky swim outfit at college, Mrs. Broadwater." She reached a hand out and took the lady's in hers. "I assure you, modesty was not compromised. However, we could swim with safety. Wouldn't that be a suitable compromise?"

The colonel stroked his manicured goatee as he thought. Then, putting a hand on his daughter's head, he said, "Miss O'Connor, would you be able to show us some of these new designs? If Mrs. Broadwater and I could take a look at them, I'd consider replacing all the rental costumes. But we still have the challenge of affordability."

The frizzy little Rapunzel tossed a conqueror's grin at Hugh. The sparkle in her amber eyes seared him like a burning beam swinging from a roof to bowl him over. An odd thought snuck up on him. If he had to work with her, he'd have to protect himself from this fiery female.

CHAPTER 3

Delphina poured over swimming costume designs in
the small salon of the Broadwater Hotel as she sipped
strong coffee from a regular china cup set marked with a
red "B". Would bare arms be more shocking than tight
fitting leggings? Could they do away with the swim slippers? That, at the very least, bringing similarity to the
German women who'd already shunned slippers to
compete.

Swimming with slippers hampered a girl as much as all
the yards of fabric. Both acted as dragging anchors in the
water. Slippers because ankles couldn't flex for a proper
propelling kick. Would she be pushing the social conven-
tions too much outside of a college setting? But Montanans
could be much more independent than society back East.
More practical in the less forgiving western frontier.

"The better choice, Miss O'Connor, is simply to stay in
the shallows."

She pressed her lips together before lifting her face to
meet Hugh Thomas' oh too practical intrusion. Time to

practice the fruits of the Spirit her mother badgered her with, though for some reason gentleness and self-control continued to elude Delphina's best intentions. Better not to alienate a co-worker, even if he was an aggravatingly opinionated male. Be nice. Be nice. She leveled her voice to something her mother would appreciate, making sure not to portray rudeness. "My father taught us all to swim before I was four. It's completely reasonable for women to be excellent swimmers."

"It may be reasonable, but it simply isn't done. Women aren't meant to do sports. They're meant to—"

"Meant to what? Women are competing in sports and excelling at them." Her better judgment flew out the window as the words flew out of her mouth. "Exactly how do you think women stay healthy? We aren't as helpless as you men want us to be, Mr. Thomas." There that ought to —my but he was a handsome man all cleaned up properly.

"Want you to be? I don't want women to be helpless." His eyes held a no-nonsense expression. "They just are. Even the Bible says—"

There he went, preaching man-speak at her again. "The Bible! How dare you throw misquoted scripture at me to prove a ridiculous misinformed, male chauvinist—"

A throat cleared, followed by a light cough, at the doorway.

Both Delphina and Hugh twisted to find their well-liked and extraordinarily respected employer studying them both.

She blushed, hating that she'd lost control of her temper again. But worse, that she'd be known for contention rather than proper manners. Why did Hugh Thomas bring out the worst in her when she'd prefer —

Delphina chanced a side-glance through her lashes at the man who seemed most capable of goading her out of a job, if she didn't stop biting his bait. The last thing she wanted right now would be taking a train back to Philadelphia a failure. Mama would be sure to marry her off the moment the train arrived. Being allowed to go to college as the youngest child had been a huge feat—then it didn't work out so well at the end.

"Miss O'Connor," Mr. Broadwater put his hands behind his back and walked over to the table. "Have you come to any decisions on appropriate swim wear for the ladies?"

He completely ignored the argument. Did that mean she'd be called into his office privately? Or would he let it go?

"Sir, I believe this outfit would be best." She shuffled a few sketches and offered a view of a fitted two-piece ensemble. The leggings stopped mid-calf and the sleeves covered the shoulders, but stopped just over the edge. "However, in light of the old-fashioned sentiments some people carry," Delphina lifted a brow at Hugh Thomas as her boss deliberated over the design. "I've also chosen two others with more tendency toward social approval." She shuffled the pages again and slipped one on either side of her favorite. Both had varying lengths of tunic skirts, sleeves, and longer trousers. None exhibited the twelve yards of fabric current swim costumes.

"I see."

Mr. Broadwater bent a balding head over the table. His non-committal response as he reviewed the designs sent a spasm of worry into her stomach. Were all three completely out of the question?

Then the last person she wanted to hear from chose to

speak. "Sir, I feel the expense is unjustified. Without the higher crowds yet coming to the natatorium, keeping the ladies in the shallow end would be much more profitable and reasonable. Certainly you can't expect every lady to purchase a new swim costume."

"No, Hugh, I don't. But I am concerned for the safety of our patrons and their perception of being limited. I believe my Julia would enjoy peace of mind as well." He patted Delphina's shoulder. "If I always worried about other people's opinions, I wouldn't have succeeded in the wilds of Montana territory before we became a state. I spent years expanding the transportation system here when most men were mining. The business is always in the supply chain. I wouldn't have built my dream resort, either. I study opinions, but I don't make my decisions based on an opinion alone."

Delphina didn't begrudge the pride and joy he displayed in the Broadwater Hotel and Natatorium. He'd earned it. Over five hundred thousand dollars went into the Moroccan architecture, landscaped grounds, and plush interior designs. The hotel and indoor swimming theatre rivaled the best the world had to offer, including the famous hot waters of Europe's Carlsbad, Bohemia.

"The best we can do is the best we can do. Nothing less." Mr. Broadwater pulled out a hanky and coughed into it. "Pardon me. I have a little throat irritation. I may need to partake of my own healing waters today." He tucked the hanky back in his pocket with a reassuring smile.

Delphina's trembling stomach eased. Everyone knew the medicinal waters improved a cold. Why, they relieved arthritis, muscle aches, and recuperated languishing limbs. He'd feel much better for the soak. It'd be a good place for him to mull over the designs she'd suggested as well.

"I believe, my dear, that you are a forward thinker, too. You believe women should have the right to swim and dress safely. Am I right?"

"Yes, sir." She grinned. "Women shouldn't be given the right to swim and dress safely." She emphasized the word "given". "We need to act on those innate rights and stop throwing them away because someone else doesn't like that they exist."

He nodded. "Well said. And do you believe, given the opportunity, that women would prefer safety over societal pressure to conform to certain fashions?"

"Sir, your wife is a suffragette, as are many of the women in Montana. From what I gather, you're very supportive of women's rights. If given the opportunity, women would very much prefer to choose their entitlement to safety and healthy exercise as freely as men do." She lifted the page corner of her first choice. "They might balk because this looks so different, but this one will help us protect swimmers while these others are better, they're not as safe. Make safer options available and they'll prefer it. Women are smart and logical."

Mr. Thomas snorted. "Logic is another topic entirely."

Placing a hand on the other man's shoulder, Mr. Broadwater observed, "It is quite different than the current styles."

"Yes, but look at this newspaper article." She held it out for both men to scan. "Women are already moving into competition using clothing similar to this design—and not only in university settings. How in the world could they compete with skirts and blouses dragging them down?"

He took the article and read it. When he finished, he laid the paper back on the table and sat in the nearby chair, signaling the others to join him.

As Delphina sat, Mr. Thomas stepped forward and held her chair. The surprise flitted across her face before she could capture it. "Thank you." Then she followed him with her gaze as he walked round to the other side. Who was he, a bore or—

"I'm still a gentleman whether we agree or not." The twinkle in his eye glimmered as the clear electric lights shimmering from the chandelier. "My concern, Miss O'Connor, isn't whether women can swim. It's the incessant risk we're taking with lives, those of the swimmers and those that save foolhardy individuals."

"I see. And you would have those risks continue when there's a way to minimize them?"

"Of course not. But you're talking a society of people used to certain fashions and that includes locals and tourists, if they begin to come. Your idea would mean a drastic shift in how our society works."

"Did you not just hear swim fashions are already changing in Europe?" She pushed the paper at him. "American fashions follow. It's easier than you think."

Mr. Broadwater held up his hand. "I believe we've established women are interested in healthy activity, and apparently competition. As the swimming instructors, I'd like to know how you both think we can overcome social pressure from those who don't believe women should wear a costume that's say…" Mr. Broadwater leaned forward and tapped the center sketch that showed a woman's calves, "less than the usual modesty?"

"We could replace the rentals all at once so there aren't any other options." Delphina suggested with a shrug.

Mr. Thomas nodded. "That would help. But you're asking Mr. Broadwater to take on a huge outlay when tourism hasn't fully developed to support that kind of investment."

"I do appreciate your concern for the resort's success, my boy, however if these are the European fashions, then all the more crucial we keep up here. We can't appear behind the times and hope to participate in the marketplace."

Delphina leaned forward in her chair. Could it be possible Mr. Broadwater would agree? "Consider the temperature of the water. With all that clothing layered on a woman's body, even those who want to stay and enjoy a bathe can't stay in the plunge for long before they're overheated."

"May I?" Mr. Broadwater held his hand out for the designs. "I'll share them with my wife and give you a decision tomorrow."

"Of course, sir." Delphina lifted the sheets and handed them to her boss. She couldn't keep her grin away if she'd tried. "I look forward to hearing your decision. I'm sure any of them will work. But I do hope she agrees with me on the most functional."

"I'll let you know right away." He nodded at both of them and slid back his chair. "Now I leave you two to get better acquainted—and build a team from here on out. The other natatorium staff watches the two of you as an example. When one allows negativity into the workplace, it's like a wave of insects that eat the crop." He gave them each an eye-to-eye silent message—and Delphina caught the meaning. *Figure out how to get along.*

But a team? What did he mean by that when there were only two people? Delphina stared after Mr. Broadwater as he sauntered across the highly polished wood floor.

"You heard the man, Miss O'Connor, we're to become a team."

"Mr. Thomas—"

"Hugh. Since we're building camaraderie."

"All right, Hugh, then." She determined to be amenable and met his first name offer with her own, plus a friendly smile. "My name is Delphina."

"Really? Where did your parents come up with a moniker like that?"

Her smile faded. "Really." She glanced out the elegantly appointed window. The paddle-boats would be much preferable to small talk with the toad that belonged in the pond. But for the sake of her position, she might as well help the toad hop into polite conversation. "My parents have eight other children. We'd moved to Philadelphia shortly before my birth and my mother loved the sense of patriotism it gave her as a new American citizen. Hence, Delphina. My name celebrates the joy of becoming Americans and I happen to be the firstborn generation."

His eyes widened. "That's an impressive legacy. I think I like your mother already."

Maybe he wasn't quite a toad then. Delphina relaxed. "Most people do. My mother is quite popular. She's kind, funny, and generous."

"Looking at her daughter, I can believe that." He leaned back into the leather chair.

Was he complementing her? "I… don't know what to say. Thank you?"

He chuckled. "It's only an honest observation. Although I don't think you intended to be funny tumbling like a newborn foal yesterday."

She gasped at his rude reference. No, he was a toad. Gentlemen did not revive a lady's embarrassing incident. "You certainly know how to add insult to injury, don't you?" She folded her arms and turned a shoulder toward him. How could they build a team if half that team couldn't manage to observe common courtesies?

"But I'd add persuasive and tenacious."

Delphina stared at Hugh. "Oh, those are admirable qualities, I'm sure."

"Wait a minute there." He reached across the table and touched Delphina's elbow. "I'm not kidding. How you held onto Wilder and wouldn't let go even if you drowned with her, well, I doubt anyone else would have gone so far. That's the stuff of heroism."

"Heroism?" Was he trying to gain back her favor for some reason? "That's not what you called it yesterday." She put a finger by her temple. "Let me see, I recall hearing irresponsible, inexperienced, and the threat that you'd have me fired."

"That was before I heard the whole story." His eyes took on a humorous glint. "And before I knew of your spinsterhood."

"I cannot believe—" She pushed back her chair and shot up.

"Whoa there, Delphina."

"I, Mr. Thomas, am not a horse, nor am I a spinster because I am not married. Do not address me in such an insulting manner." Delphina whirled in a swish of her A-line, navy blue skirt and started for the carved pocket door. She'd escape this hooligan's presence until her temper eased and she could forgive. Though that might be awhile as he kept transgressing. Lord, your seventy times seven plan seems to be this man's favorite pastime. How am I supposed to work with a constantly croaking toad? A man that attractive should have warts the size of his insults to warn unsuspecting—

"Wait, let me explain—"

Delphina stopped and glared over her shoulder, "If you were a gentleman, it would be an apology." As she raised her skirt, and turned to leave, she glanced back at the sound of footsteps behind her. She picked up her pace and faced forward too late. The next moment, she staggered backward from the impact between the door and her head. The room spun as black spots widened and engulfed Delphina in the sensation of rushing to the floor.

CHAPTER 4

WATCHING HER EYELIDS FLUTTER, Hugh released the breath he held. She had to be the most accident-prone woman he'd ever met. Catching her in his arms broke her fall. But the egg on her forehead would give her a headache the size of nearby Mount Helena. Still, he wanted to see the fire in Delphina's eyes again. They sparked a simmer in his veins. He carried her to the horsehair sofa near the wall opposite the large wall in the salon.

Her eyes blinked up into his.

"Hi, how are you feeling?" He kept his volume low in case loud noises hurt.

She flinched anyway and lifted a hand to touch the knot. "What happened?"

"Uh, we were displaying less than courteous behavior." He cleared his throat and raised a brow. "Evidently there were guests in the lobby."

"I ran into a guest?" Her smooth forehead crinkled.

He laughed. "Oh, sorry." Hugh offered at her wince. "No, the door."

"The door?" She craned her neck to see around Hugh. "That's a three hundred pound slab of wood!"

"It's a bit tougher than you, I'd say. You didn't even leave a dent." He hovered a finger above her brow. "Except there." He caught her confused gaze.

"But it was open." Delphina raised a hand to touch the growing egg. "Ooh, ow!"

"The desk clerk slid it closed to keep our conversation quiet. I tried to catch you, but—" he shrugged. With a tinge of humor he said, "I guess there's no limit on how many times a fellow can be a hero around you."

She grimaced.

"Holding you in my arms three times in the space of a few days, I may get lonesome if you—" Hugh caught himself. For some reason he didn't want to introduce the idea of another man in Delphina's life. Not with the vast opportunity in Helena.

"Am I going to fall?"

"What?"

"Fall. Am I in jeopardy of falling?"

"No, of course not."

"Then why haven't you released me?" She pushed against his bicep. "This is most unbecoming. What if someone saw me in this… this predicament?"

Hugh didn't want to, but he gently slid his arm out from under her back and lowered her head to the curved sofa arm, then slid his hand out from behind her soft hair and the warm, velvety skin at the nape of her neck. "Someone already has."

Delphina struggled to her elbow and pressed the other hand to her stomach as she waited out a wave of nausea.

She still managed to grit out, "You can't be serious. Why would you put me in such a situation?"

That sparkling spirit in her eyes hit Hugh hard in the gut. To have an intelligent, exciting woman like this fall for him would be much preferable to society's vision of womanhood. Of course, she held the trump card in that deck statistically. Was she aware she could snap her fingers and men a hundred deep would line up for the chance at a wife where there were so few? He wanted to stoke the sparks he felt building between them as much as he wanted her to trust him. Which she didn't—yet.

"My first impression of you is accurate. You are not a gentleman."

"I promise you, Delphina, I am. I merely sent Frankie for some ice."

"The fact that you goaded me into danger doesn't factor in for you, does it?"

Hugh backed away from the sofa. Better to give a wide berth than take on the whole hive. The queen bee did have several reasons to sting right now, even though he'd meant well. As the natatorium manager, and the head swimming instructor, he hadn't given her his trust either. But then, being surprised with a new employee in the middle of a double drowning wasn't the way he normally did business. The colonel seemed to be slipping after his bout with influenza a few weeks ago. Since Hugh hadn't known, did Delphina realize who her supervisor was?

"I think due to our unusual introduction we might be better served to start again."

She lay back on the curved velvet sofa arm. Dropping a hand over her eyes, she waved a hand. "How about we try that tomorrow? I think I've had about as much of you as I can take today."

No, she couldn't have a clue. "Tomorrow it is."

"I chipped some fresh ice from the pond, Mr. Thomas." Frankie held out a tea towel wrapped in a knotted packet. "Good thing it's been cold still in the mornings."

"Well done." He took it and transferred it to Delphina's head, taking care not to cause undue pain. Then, placing her hand over the ice as her mouth pursed, he let go and said, "Keep this over that knot, and please don't go swimming for a day or two, especially not the deep end."

She attempted to swing her legs to the floor. Then her face scrunched into a wince. "I will swim when I'm ready to swim and if I want to swim in the deep end, I will."

He sighed, his next words were about to loose the hive. "No, you won't. As your supervisor, I need you to see the physician this afternoon and wait for his clearance before resuming your duties or going in the plunge at all. Then we'll—"

"My what?" Delphina's eyes grew as big as the formal dining room's china platters as she dropped the ice. Slapping it back on her bump a bit too fast, she grunted out, "Ow!"

He shook his head. "Until tomorrow."

CHAPTER 5

THE NATATORIUM'S walls rang with the laughter of the boys' swim team. Hugh paced the deck, no jacket or tie, sleeves rolled up, watching as more boys slapped the wall finishing laps. "Ten minutes, then off with you all home."

Delphina stood at the side rail. A few minutes splashing about anywhere in the pool they chose, completely free. How could she gain the same freedoms for the girls she would train if they couldn't have simple swim garb? Waiting on the final decision gave her as much of a headache as the purple lump on her head.

One of the boys swam near the plunge railing and waved. "How are you feeling, Miss O'Connor?"

"Frankie, right?"

"Right-o."

"I didn't have the chance to thank you yesterday for bringing me the packet of ice."

Frankie caught the edge of the pool and swung himself up in a lithe leap. "Just hopin' you're gettin' well." He swiped a soggy lock out of his eyes. "Looked like you got a good wallop. Mighta been worse if Mr. Thomas hadn't caught ya'."

"Mr. Thomas caught me?"

"Yeah, sure he did. I done heard a big thump then Mr. Thomas yelled for help." He grabbed the towel draped nearby. "Don't mean no disrespect, but he had hold of you pretty good."

"Oh." That would explain why she didn't have a matching set of lumps. Delphina raised fingertips and touched the back of her head, grateful for its normalcy. The possibility hadn't occurred to her. "No offense taken. In fact, I need to thank Mr. Thomas for his quick reflexes then, don't I? But first, thank you for yours."

"I was just comin' in to tell him we have another fella gonna take lifesaving class." Frankie looked at his feet. "Not meanin' to bring up yer bad luck, ma'am, but savin' two lives the other day is kind of gittin' around."

Delphina cringed. "Yes, I'm quite sure it's big news around town already."

Frankie didn't say anything. His discomfort said it all.

"It's all right, Frankie. I'll live through a little gossip" She pushed through her misgivings. Gossip. The reason her parents allowed their youngest child to venture to Montana to let it all die down. Even with her education degree, folks didn't consider it proper behavior to swim competitively at the age a woman should be married and having babies. It didn't help that she'd borrowed her brother's swim team uniform and raced against one of the leading male swim-mers. She had not been indecent. The dark cotton blouse tucked under it kept her modesty. Unfortunately, the dean did not agree. If only she'd won! Although a second from winning proved she swam faster than most of the young men on the team. The challenge hadn't been a sanctioned activity. Though the college awarded her diploma, banning her from walking in the commencement exercise still stuck under Delphina's ribs—shaming the O'Connor family. The women's uniforms were progressive, but the skirts and slippers still held her back in the water. All she wanted to do was prove women could swim fast and have fun competing. Wearing the shorter skirts in practice seemed to add strength and speed when unfettered by them during the race. The even longer skirts still worn by women, with twelve yards of merino wool down to her ankles, blousy sleeves, and laced-up slippers—how could any intelligent human being wrap women in these death traps?

"Frankie, may I buy you and your friends some treats? I would like to offer a more tangible form of appreciation than mere words."

"Nah, we're just glad you and Miss Wilder are both doing so good."

Delphina smiled. "I saw her a few moments ago, and yes, she's also recovered nicely."

Frankie ducked his head, but his grin couldn't be wider.

Did he have a crush on the budding Miss Wilder Broadwater?

"Off to the shower, Frankie. Your folks expect you and your brothers home in time for dinner. I hear you have company tonight." Hugh joined them.

"Yes, sir!" He hurried to change.

"Delphina, good to see you up and about."

"Thank you." She gestured at the disappearing boy. "He's sure a nice young man. His parents have raised him well."

"He's only had parents for about two years. Evan and

Mirielle Rutherford adopted Frankie when he and his crew found Mr. Rutherford's missing son. Now they provide a home to the rest of the newsies when the boarding school closes during the holidays and summer."

"The newsies?"

"Eleven boys who sold papers for the Helena Independent in the streets." He shrugged. "To be fair, I think our whole town has adopted them."

"You're telling me Mr. and Mrs. Rutherford now have eleven sons?"

"And a new little daughter."

She swallowed. "A dozen children?" She squeaked out. Then shook her head. "I don't know if I ever want even one."

Shock registered on his handsome features. "You don't want children? Who ever heard of a woman that didn't want—"

"I told you once, I am not a horse. Women do not have to bear children to be worthy." Then she closed her eyes. Why couldn't she keep her own counsel? Especially when the reason she came to see Hugh wasn't to argue women's rights or place in society. She'd meant to convey deep gratitude, not level him with personal choices he had nothing to do with. She opened her eyes. His mouth pressed into a tight, silent line. "I am so sorry. That's not at all what I wanted to say to you today."

"By all means, enlighten me." He folded his arms. "What more do I need to learn about you, Miss O'Connor?"

Her temper only barely controlled, Delphina shook her head. "I said I'm sorry."

"Apology accepted." His monotone voice and shuttered expression said otherwise.

What had he said yesterday? Start over? All right, she'd take his advice. Taking a deep breath, she stuck out a hand. "Hello, I'm Delphina O'Connor. I'm the new women's swimming instructor."

Hugh's arms dropped as his eyes opened wider.

"And you would be?" For one long moment, Delphina worried he wouldn't meet her halfway.

Then a large hand engulfed her smaller one. "Hello, I'm Hugh Thomas, the natatorium manager and men's swimming instructor." His bemused expression deepened into a full on grin.

Delphina had no idea how long they studied one another. Time seemed to stand still. Then a trickle of sound broke the moment.

"I said, I'm pleased to meet you."

Did his voice sound a bit on the husky side? "Uh, yes, uh… it's a pleasure." What was that? When did she ever have a problem with confidence? Delphina slid her hand away.

But he caught her fingertips. "May I show you around?" Hugh tucked her hand in the crook of his elbow on warm, masculine muscles.

Delphina's glance down turned into a stare at the physical contact. She'd walked with her hand on a man's arm before, but never a bare arm. Never so personal. She lifted her gaze and collided with his. The flash deep in those blue eyes stopped Delphina's heart for a split-second. "I…" What was she going to say? Certainly not that embarrassing squeak. "You don't dress to swim with the boys?"

"Not today." He kept the intimacy of a face-to-face

conversation. "I have meetings so I had them swim laps for endurance."

"Oh." He did look quite approachable without a jacket and just his tie.

"Don't get me wrong. If I saw a problem, I could dive in right away." He drew her attention downward to his bare feet and wiggled his toes. "But Frankie is my strongest swimmer. He'd likely get to a boy before I did, like the other day with Wilder."

"Frankie pulled Wilder out?"

"He's the one who heard you scream for help. I had just walked onto the deck when I saw him dive in."

"I am so glad he did."

Hugh stared into Delphina's eyes. "Me too," he said as a slow smile spread across his lips.

"Excellent. I see you're getting along well."

Hugh answered Mr. Broadwater for the both of them, "I do believe we are, sir." Then he broke eye contact. "I was about to show Miss O'Connor around our facility. Would you care to join us?"

Delphina pulled her hand back. "I'm sure I'll enjoy learning where everything is and how it all works, but I would first like to hear the answer about our women's swimming costumes." Would she stay if the answer wasn't to her liking? "Will we be able to replace them?"

"Well, my dear, we have a dilemma to solve."

"A dilemma?"

"The funds are rather tight at the moment. As much as I would like to update our selection, I'm concerned the cost would cause a problem for the resort."

"But sir, the safety issues must far outweigh the financial risk." Delphina pressed the issue. "Surely we can begin stocking a few at a time at least?"

"Hence the reason I suggested we solve the dilemma. Because something is difficult doesn't mean it's impossible."

Hugh nodded with great seriousness. "Shall we tour first? You never know when an idea will strike."

Tour? He made it sound more like a Sunday stroll. If she didn't show simple camaraderie, Mr. Broadwater wouldn't want to keep her in this new position. How long could it take? "Lead the way."

Thirty minutes later, Delphina could find every lifesaving device, changing room upper and lower levels, and where all the wooden pipes ran through the massive building.

The domed ceiling reminded her of a ship, more so the ark, with the rectangular central windows lacing the length of the building, above the pool. The boulders stacked in the deep end lavished the pool with a waterfall. Peaceful trickling over the rocks from both hot and cold springs relaxed all who swam in the warm waters. The electric lighting behind the main waterfall gave a stunning effect. The stained glass washed colorful designs that reflected on and in the water like the aurora borealis when it baptized Helena on rare occasions.

As the trio ended their explorations, Mr. Broadwater brought up the swimming dresses. "Until we have a better solution—"

No, don't say it. Delphina squeezed her hands together.

"It appears we must set the issue aside."

Delphina stopped walking as they passed the rental

desk. "What if we could redesign those that we already have?"

Mr. Broadwater stopped and walked back over to Delphina, who sat in the sales chair. "Go ahead, tell me more."

"We have all this excess yardage of thin, black material at our fingertips. Per outfit." She pulled out a skirt. "That's enough to make two outfits without skirting."

"We must be sure women will wear them. In the meantime, we have to offer something."

"Do we rent out all the outfits every day?"

"No, of course not, but how would we provide anything if we're cutting up all the attire?"

"Let's start with ten swim dresses. If we're careful, and make at least two swimming costumes out of each one, very shortly we'll have caught up to the regular rental rate. We rotate the outfits back into availability. Each time we only take ten. The ladies will have time to get familiar with the new style."

The dawning on Mr. Broadwater's face melded into an approving respect. "That, Miss O'Connor, is brilliant."

"You think so?" She pinked at his compliment.

Hugh added, "That would double the costume rental if we could gain more bathers." Then he doused the idea in ice water. "But the problem we have is getting enough bathers to come as it is."

"If women felt they had more opportunity, more of their rights recognized, they'd come." Delphina suggested. "I could put out an announcement that we're updating the design."

"Delphina," Hugh held up a hand. "This is about

building a swimming business, not the suffrage movement."

"No, you're missing the point, Mr. Thomas. Women want opportunity. Opportunity to enjoy physical fitness, competition, and making choices that benefit not only our families, yes also our country." Her words sped as passion fueled them. "Being forced to wear death traps because that's all we have to offer takes away the opportunity to make smart choices. Choices you men can make every day!"

"You think a swimming get-up will change the world?" Hugh's disbelief dulled the timbre of his deep voice. "Women have worn what women want to wear for centuries, and that includes what they wear to swim."

"Oh, you think so, do you?" She yanked the dress off the peg. "Men have forced women to cover up for centuries. It's not about fashion. It's about keeping a woman in her place, milk toast and controlled!"

Mr. Broadwater started coughing. He dug a hanky out and covered his mouth with the other hand held up for quiet.

All of a sudden, Delphina realized she'd gone too far. Why did she have such an intense desire to win an argument with this man? So much for starting over. But Mr. Broadwater's coughing escalated. It didn't appear to be a guise to halt her faux pas.

"Sir? Do you need a glass of water?" Delphina offered.

Hugh's face looked worried. "I'll get it."

"Give me a moment," Mr. Broadwater rasped.

Hugh returned as Delphina walked with the resort owner to a nearby sitting area. "This should help a bit."

The older man nodded his appreciation and sipped at

the healing mineral waters. "Sorry to trouble you two. This cold doesn't want to let go." He coughed a few more times. "My wife is beside herself since I just got over the influenza." He smiled. "You'd think I was a two-day-old kitten the way she wants to coddle me." Mr. Broadwater seemed over the spell.

The peaceful moment gave her the chance to apologize. "I'm terribly sorry for being rude, gentlemen. That's truly not my intent."

Hugh swung to look at her as he took the seat beside Mr. Broadwater on the wood and wrought-iron bench. "I haven't made it easy for you. But I hope you understand I'm not trying to limit women at all. My concern, as manager, is to make sure we begin to make a profit while maintaining a safe recreational area."

Mr. Broadwater agreed and tucked the handkerchief away. "I'm afraid the crowds I expected haven't materialized. I was sure once the rails went in we'd have more traffic from the East than we could handle." He stared out at the nearly empty plunge. "As much as I want to do exactly as you request, Miss O'Connor, this venture hasn't yet operated at a profit."

"What if we could attract more women through this change? Would it be worth it?"

"You have a good mind, Miss O'Connor." Mr. Broadwater tapped his fingers on his knee. "You are a creative problem solver and you think about how these things will affect the future." He turned to include Hugh. "You, young man, are trustworthy and reliable." He waggled a finger between the two of them. "Together, I have a team that can bring success to this business now and into the future. That is why I chose each of you. For your strengths. Now, rather than fighting about money, I suggest the two of you use your strengths to bring the solution into being and more people into the resort. I do believe it's possible."

Hugh looked as chastised as Delphina felt. "You mean with my idea remaking the outfits?"

"Who knows if you're ahead of your time? It's a valuable idea. Let's see if it might help us now." He bobbled a little as he rose. "I'll leave you to come up with a plan so that I don't have to close the natatorium down." He scanned the massive aqua theatre. "I had a big dream. Maybe I, too, am ahead of my time."

CHAPTER 6

HUGH WATCHED the colonel walk out the door. "Something's not quite right. Not just his cough." The door closed behind his boss and mentor. "Do you notice his lack of energy?"

Delphina drew her brows together and nodded. "I only met him a few weeks ago, but I agree. I see a difference. Though having a cold can drag it out of a person."

"Let's hope that's all it is. I have the greatest respect for that man. He's built transportation companies, banks, and railroads—all extremely successful. I know he can make the Hotel Broadwater and Natatorium successful as well. He just needs a little more time."

"He's built railroads?"

"You know the trolley line into town belongs to him, right?"

"Of course, but I didn't realize how many other endeavors he'd achieved."

Hugh became animated in his admiration. "Without Charles A. Broadwater, Helena and Montana wouldn't be the modern Queen City of the Rockies that she is. When I said transportation companies, I meant with his efforts, the infrastructure within our great state became a reality. He started as a superintendent with the Diamond R Freighting Company. Then he moved the home base here to Helena and bought the company with three friends."

"So he went from an employee to an owner." Delphina studied the incredible design of the building they sat in. "From modest beginnings to such a lavish resort, his vision coupled with business acumen makes him a rare man."

"That's not all of the colonel's accomplishments."

"Colonel?"

"An honorary title the army bestowed for his patriotic acts, supplying the troops at Fort Assiniboine and Fort Maginnis. He owned a trading store and never overcharged. Charles Broadwater is known for his honesty, courtesy, and generosity. After founding the store, he opened the Montana National Bank."

"Astonishing! One wouldn't expect a resume like that from such a kind, unassuming man."

"He has no need to impress. His example does that for him." Hugh glanced at the door. "If I can be half of that, I'd consider myself an overwhelming success." He shook his head. "But even half of that is more than most men can hope to be in a lifetime."

"I understand why you'd want to mentor under such an accomplished entrepreneur."

"Yes, I came on board just prior to our grand opening. Five hundred people attended."

"My goodness, that's a huge party."

"Not large enough, unfortunately. One of the reasons the colonel's investments thrive is his ability to prospect in business the way other men mine gold. He has a knack for knowing where to dig for business gold. This resort, however, may not pan out." Hugh ran a hand over the back of his neck. "Some mines cave in. It's just so unusual for Broadwater to be wrong." He stopped and thought. "I hope the stress of potential failure isn't adding to his load."

"What do you mean? It's popular and there's a constant flow of visitors." Delphina motioned at the plunge, where quite a few bathers frolicked with their children. The waterfall, forty feet of stacked boulders, rained two lovely terrace cliffs into the pool below. The back lit waterfalls and their glowing reflections mesmerized her each time she walked into the aquatic theater. The playful spray fountain in the center created constant squeals of glee. Surely it would continue to build in reputation and attendance.

"The Broadwater was built to become the greatest resort in the world. Five hundred people are a small percentage of what she can host. With fifty rooms, the grounds, the natatorium, and the many outdoor recreation opportunities we should have overflowed." He saw the dawning in Delphina's eyes. "Only thirty-five were booked for one night."

"And so, asking for new swim costumes truly is a drain on constrained resources." Delphina's eyes filled and she dipped her head as she rolled her thumbs around one another in her lap. "Then how do we find a way, as Mr. Broadwater has asked us to do?"

"Your idea does have merit. We need to be diligent about the research so we don't stumble in the execution and cost our employer more money. For instance, would other women feel the way you do? Would that help us build clientele or would it drive us into lower attendance at the natatorium? If we go forward, what's the least expensive option while producing quality that won't require constant replenishment?"

"Might I suggest I do a little research this week?"

No arguments? No reasoning him around to her way of thinking? She could raise his hackles faster than a coyote snatches a chicken, but their conversations left him invigorated rather than irritated. Other women he'd met didn't have the confidence to stand up for their beliefs. She had confidence, courage, and candor.

"The physician will not allow me to enter the water or take on my classes for another week. I disagree, however, who am I to challenge a doctor?" She sat back in her spot on the bench. "But I can't expect Mr. Broadwater to pay me for doing nothing. Since we need more information, I'll earn my keep by obtaining it."

Delphina's resilience attracted him more than the beauty of her face and figure. He liked looking at her, no doubt. But the confidence that sparkled in her eyes and the way she carried herself drew him. Beautiful, yes, because of the energy and presence about her. Nothing seemed too big of a challenge. If David facing the giant had been a woman, she'd have been Delphina. And weren't they facing a giant now with a half-a-million dollar business on the line?

If Hugh wanted to find a woman of substance, someone he could talk with, build a friendship like he saw between the Broadwaters, someone who intrigued him, then Delphina O'Connor definitely met that criteria. She fearlessly shared ideas and opinions. Even more, with her on his team, Hugh's confidence grew. A woman like that, who inspired him and believed all things possible, she'd be the kind of wife to help him build his dreams. But could he help build hers?

This suffragette created fireworks in his blood. Hugh tugged at his collar. Then he smiled to himself. At the rate Miss Delphina O'Connor was going, he'd have to make sure she lived so he could court her. But she seemed quite content without a husband, without children. Hugh never envisioned a future family life without children. Asking to court her would be fruitless. Unless she changed her mind...

Hugh stood and offered a hand to Delphina. So far, the last few minutes were the most amenable they'd had. Did he want her to change her mind?

Delphina touched his palm and triggered an instantaneous thumping in his chest.

Oh yes. He'd find a way to bring her around. That thump grew to a thundering gallop.

CHAPTER 7

THE FRESH SPRING air tickled across Delphina's face as she waited for the trolley into town. She fashioned her hair as far forward as possible and tipped her wide-brimmed hat slightly to hide the two-day-old dark purple bruise, now yellowing around the edges but not faded enough.

Hugh tapped her shoulder and stepped up beside her on the lawn near the trolley rail. "May I join you on your mission today?"

"That's a funny thing to call business with a seamstress shop." She smiled. "I'm just taking one of the swim dresses to see what it would cost to remake them or use the excess material to create the new ones."

"Downtown then?"

She nodded. "Yes, and I hear there are a few seamstresses in Reeder's Alley that might be willing to work less per piece if I can guarantee quantity."

"Then I'll definitely accompany you."

"Oh?"

"That area can be a bit rough for a lady these days. It's becoming mostly, well," he shrugged.

"I see. But you don't have to curtail the business you've planned in town. I'm sure I'll be fine."

He looked down the track as the trolley came into view. "You are my business in town."

Did his voice soften just then? Delphina cocked her head. What did he mean, she was his business?

Hugh glanced from the trolley's arrival to Delphina's confusion. "You do remember we're a team, don't you?"

"Of course. But—" she squinted against the sun in the blue, blue sky and raised a hand to block the brightness. For a cold winter morning, the sun didn't seem to believe he should be in hiding with spring around the corner. It seemed like the coming spring had an embrace waiting.

"Even managers get a day off. I saw you heading into town with the large bag and thought I might help you." He held out his hand for the valise. "May I?"

"You followed me?"

"No, I happened to be heading into town to do my banking. But if you don't mind, I'd be honored to accompany you on your errand. The faster we get the answers, the faster we're able to help Colonel Broadwater turn the resort into a success."

She couldn't argue with his logic. Nor should she after agreeing to work as a team. "All right, then. I plan to get more than one estimate." She controlled the grin that wanted to break loose at his surprised expression. "I'll also want to see some of the seamstresses projects to prove workmanship."

"What you're telling me is that this is a longer expedition?" His lips twitched. "Possibly into the dinner hour?"

"I wouldn't think it need go that long." Maybe men did think with their stomachs. She couldn't stop the grin. "But should you need sustenance, then I'll be happy to release you from escorting me."

The trolley's passengers streamed off into the grounds in various directions. Hugh climbed up the steps and held his palm up to assist Delphina. "Should we need sustenance, and I hope we do, it would be my pleasure to invite you to share dinner with me."

Delphina's hand fluttered and stopped mid-air. "Mr. Thomas, I did not finagle to get an invitation to dinner." The whistle blew. The trolley would leave without her if she didn't hurry. She landed her hand in his and raised her skirts as she stepped up, then settled in the bench for the trip to town. Glad she'd chosen the lavender walking suit that made her feel more confident. The jacket tailored perfectly to her pleat at her hips, where the matching skirt moved smartly at the ankle, but didn't drag beyond her favorite kid leather boots.

"No, Miss O'Connor, it was I that hoped to finagle you into dining with me."

"I'm sure it won't be necessary." She peeked at him sideways. "But thank you, just the same."

He faced forward and gave a sidelong glance with a mischievous smile. "Ah, but I hope it is necessary. We should get to know one another better, don't you think?"

"We have the beginnings of a good working relationship."

"Exactly." As he set the carpetbag down beside her lavender and white striped walking skirt, he added, "the beginnings. We need to work in unison, as one. You should know me well enough to not only support my decisions, but to make the kind of decision I would make should that need arise. I should know you well enough to understand any decision you would need to make on behalf of your students and the resort. This is all for the good of everyone, you know. If the resort fails, imagine how many people would be out of work. We just can't let that happen as the two people who Colonel Broadwater counts on, can we?"

She swallowed. He made it abundantly clear. Hugh Thomas would be involved every step of the way. "Why are you so passionate about the Broadwater's success?"

"I'm an investor. I want the resort to succeed for all of us, not just myself."

"I had no idea you were personally invested. It makes sense that you feel so strongly about the future of the business."

"Delphina, I believe in the vision and future of the hotel and resort. So do a lot of other people. Montana's silver brings new residents while building for future tourism brings the foundation for financial stability. You must believe it also or you wouldn't be here." He stopped talking and turned to her. "Why did you come all the way from Philadelphia?"

"I have an uncle and his family out here. My parents allowed me to answer the advertisement from the Hotel Broadwater for a female swimming instructor because I'd have family to watch out for me."

"You don't strike me as someone who'd need permission to do whatever you want to do."

"Is that an insult?"

"Not at all." He looked puzzled. "I meant you know your own mind."

Then why didn't she right now? Sitting this close, Delphina could feel the warmth of his arm and became acutely aware of her own shortness of breath.

"I find that characteristic unusual in both men and women."

"You do?"

"Doesn't it annoy you? Everyone is so busy deferring answers that conversation can't ever go anywhere?" He clasped his hands together between his knees. "It's like no one can think for themselves. They're too busy being careful and polite. How will we grow and change as a society if we can't talk courteously about real issues?"

"Every time I say anything I tend to cause an uproar, according to my parents." She gave him a conspiratorial smile. "Evidently, I have the inability to maintain a peaceful, civilized repartee. My mother says it's the gift of advocacy. But then I didn't help things along last spring when I raced against a boy at college."

He stared at her. "Did you win?" he finally asked.

"One arm stroke behind."

"I'll remember that next time I hop in a pool with you nearby." He winked. "My boys might be tough to teach if—"

"You don't believe me?"

"Thing is, Delphina, I do." The trolley came to the end of the electric line and stopped. Hugh picked up the bag and held out his hand to help her slide out of the wooden bench. "Shall we?"

A warmth rushed over her. Hugh hadn't minimized her for the loss or the action. Maybe they could grow to like one another after all. She looked at his dark brown, curly hair and profile. He seemed strong and kind and genuine.

Quite handsome, too. But the man who'd jilted her for the gossip had been quite handsome. He didn't like her speaking her mind, either. Another quick perusal at his face as she stepped down to the street level. Hugh never failed to act the gentleman and he'd heard her speak her mind.

THREE SHOPS AND ESTIMATIONS LATER, Hugh ushered Delphina into a café on Last Chance Gulch. "Why don't we consider our notes and options over a good meal?" The luscious scent of roasted chicken and freshly baked apple pie wafted over them as they entered. He'd have loved to take Delphina to a much nicer establishment, but she agreed to a casual setting. She continued to surprise him, liking simplicity over extravagance. With the wealth continuing to build in Helena, finding anyone enjoying a more simple life was getting harder.

"I could use a little food." She inhaled and closed her eyes. "Mmm, that smells delicious."

The pleasure on her face enjoying simple apple pie aromas struck Hugh. He couldn't take his eyes off her. When she opened her eyes, the sparkle of joy about knocked him flat.

"I don't care if I eat a meal, but I'd really like a piece of that pie."

He swallowed in order to answer her. "I'll buy the whole pie for you."

She laughed. "No, that won't be necessary."

He held her chair as she sat. Draping her the light wrap over the neighboring chair, he slid his hat onto the seat as well. "Would you like more than dessert? It's been a long time since breakfast."

The smile she bestowed on him grew slowly until she held him mesmerized. "It hasn't felt like it." Delphina's stomach growled. "But then again…" She pressed her hand into her abdomen. She leaned in and whispered, "It might be a smart plan."

Was she feeling the connection between them, too? "I do want you to see me as a smart man. Chicken dinner and pie?"

"Perfect."

He called the waitress over. "We can think of nothing better at this moment than to order your chicken dinner with the pie for dessert."

"Some reason, that's all we're sellin' at the moment." She gave them both a friendly smile and went to place their order.

"Would there be enough funding to start with the ten swimming costumes I suggested?"

Hugh calculated his budget. "I'm sorry to say I don't think so."

She looked crestfallen. "Then there's nothing we can do?"

He shook his head. "I hate to spoil our dinner, but I don't see how."

"I won't be able to teach successfully relegated to the shallow end. You know that."

"I know. But without the funds to match any of the esti-mates, we can't take the risk. We have payroll to make—and not just yours and mine. We have the staff to think about."

The waitress delivered roasted chicken, green beans, mashed potatoes covered in creamy brown gravy, and buttermilk biscuits slathered with butter.

"I'd need an entire team to finish this plate." Delphina's eyes stared at the heaping servings. "Wait." She looked up from the mountain of steaming potatoes. "A team. That's it!"

"What's it? Our team can't sew."

"No, they don't need to sew." She giggled at him, raising his spirits. "We start with the girls. The families have the funds for the swimming costumes. If we create a reason to need them quickly, say a water pageant, we could provide the pattern and all three seamstresses as references to have the costumes made."

"A water pageant?"

"One of my duties is to teach ornamental swimming. How better to build interest in the opportunities at the natatorium than a water pageant?"

Their chicken cooled in front of them. But the excite-ment of the idea built. Hugh realized Delphina stumbled on a bigger solution than just the women's costume dilemma. She'd found a way to bring in repeat crowds.

"With water pageants, we can hold regular events from recitals to bigger extravaganzas." Hugh grasped her hand and kissed it. "You, Delphina, are brilliant!"

"I only thought of a pageant to start the change in fash-ion. You thought of the rest."

"But I couldn't have without you." He hadn't let go of

her hand. Now he covered it with his other one. "How long would it take to build an entertaining presentation?"

"If we give the seamstresses time to make the more simple costumes for the girls, I could put a show together in a couple of months with three practices a week.

"What if we planned an event for May Day?"

"If we work together, hold an open house for the parents, and allow the families to use their own seamstresses, we could start in the shallow end learning the basic floats. By the time their new outfits are ready, we could move to the deeper water safely."

Hugh maneuvered their hands into a handshake and held them over the table. "I'll work as hard as I can to make this happen, including getting you some live musicians."

"You could do that?"

"You bet I can. How do you feel about a pipe and drum corps?" He smiled into her eyes. "Do we have a deal?"

"Absolutely." She started the handshake and they accidentally bopped the top of his potatoes. "Oops," Delphina pressed a finger against her mouth, obviously trying not to burst out giggling. But the corners of her lips flickered, as did the humor in her eyes.

He broke their handshake and tasted it. "That's good gravy. I was about to pass out from starvation." Hugh wiped away the mess as they laughed together. "Please, eat. We have a short time to get our plans in motion."

Delphina slid her warm apple pie in front of her dinner plate. "Then I vote we eat our dessert first."

Could there be a more perfect woman? Any man would —Hugh sat up tall and looked around the restaurant. Though more women populated Helena, Montana in the last few years, men still vastly outnumbered marriageable females. A pretty woman could cause a stir anywhere she went. Since she'd arrived, Delphina hadn't been out and about to garner much notice. Until today—he'd brilliantly assisted his competition. He scanned the room. Easily two-thirds men. Too many heads tipped in their direction. Delphina had caused a stir…

Hugh raised his hand to signal the waitress. "Check!"

CHAPTER 9

THE GIRLS FROM TWO CLASSES, the little ones aged six to ten, and the older girls, ages eleven to sixteen, lined up for the dress rehearsal. They'd practice together for the early segment of the ornamental water pageant and then the older girls would morph into their own recital while the women's newly formed team joined them on the edge of the plunge. But the first thirty minutes today belonged to the younger gals.

Delphina walked barefooted along the wooden plank, complimenting each girl. Their knee-length jumpsuits skimmed, but didn't hug too tightly, much like her new outfit. The black merino wool sported three black nautical stripes on a wide, white V-neck collar sewn onto the button-down blouse. The short sleeves didn't restrict arm movement. Two stripes ringed around the cuffs and the leggings gathered just below the knee. Instead of beribboned sashes, each girl wore a slim knit belt around her waist with a decorative button—and no stockings or slippers. The costume gave enough room for the routine's maneuvers while safe and modest. Delphina spoke with all the parents, female participants, and many guests. She managed to convince everyone slippers were meant for beaches, not indoor swimming pools.

As teacher and ornamental swimming team coach, Delphina offered an encouragement to each of her students. "You look so nice, Mary." She plucked a six-year-old Eugenia, whose name was bigger than the little girl, off the metal railing. "Let's be a lady now." Then she waved at the little girl's mother above on the observation deck. "She'll be fine, don't worry."

"Miss O'Connor?"

The nine-year-old's Irish lilt gave Delphina a sense of homesickness for her family. "Yes, Lea?" She bent down and put her hands on her knees, leaning into talk to the child.

"My mama says she'll bring cookies for a reception after we recite."

Delphina enjoyed getting to know Lea's mother, Calista Shanahan. They'd hit it off. Calista wasn't afraid to make choices different than the norm either, something they admired in one another.

The titters and giggles added a frivolity to the excitement building.

Lea rocked forward and back, rolling heel to toe. Then she cupped a small hand around her teacher's ear and whispered, "I'll ask her for frosted ginger ones. They're my favorite."

"Oh, what a lovely idea." Delphina thought for a moment. A reception usually followed music recitals. She glanced at the boys setting out chairs near the candy shop. This aquatic theatre would host both a water dance and concert. Didn't they all deserve a recital party after? "How many of you would like to bring cookies or treats for a reception tomorrow evening?"

Every little girl's hand shot into the air. A light buzz from the watching mothers floated down to the fidgety girls covering them all in happy sweetness. Most of the mothers signaled their approval.

"How wonderful. It's settled then. I'll be sure to let Mr. Thomas know we'll need a salon in the hotel." He'd been acting as an assistant lifeguard since their show grew to so many participants.

"He's there." Lea called out.

"Where?"

"Here." He spoke over her shoulder.

She startled and jumped backward into him, landing her bare foot on his instep.

He hopped around as if she'd broken his leg, making nonsense sounds to the delight of the children.

"I'm so sorry." Delphina raised her hands to her warming cheeks. But as she realized his antics escalated, she folded her arms and made a show of staring at the ceiling.

Then Hugh, feeding off the giggles of her team, hammed it up as if he were a peg-legged pirate. "Ahoy, me maties, I fear I've been harpooned!" He stumbled and zig-zagged over to one of the wooden slat benches against the wall and spent the longest time play-acting a beleaguered death at the hands of a mutinous first-mate. By the time he'd finally collapsed dramatically for the fourth time, half on and half off the bench, little girls were gasping for air, they'd been laughing so hard. "Blub, blub, blub. At last, my fate is sealed."

Delphina echoed, "At last."

He opened one eye in a quick peek.

"Oh no, you don't, pirate. We have a rehearsal—"

His impromptu audience burst into applause. "More, more!"

Sauntering over, Delphina couldn't help but join in the tragic comedy. If not, she might not gain control over the group again. She placed a foot over his chest and clasped her hands above her head. "I claim victory!" One more win couldn't hurt after the croquet game she'd beat him at the other day.

Even the observation deck joined in the clapping as Hugh disengaged himself and jumped up. He grabbed hold of Delphina's hand and they bowed like two thespians on stage.

Delphina tossed him a happy smile as she whispered, "Now scootch." They did make a good team in both work and play. A team engineered by Mr. Broadwater. Did he see something in them—as a couple? She snuck another glance. Did she? A flutter tickled in her stomach. She might.

"AND THAT, ladies, is entertainment. Just have fun and your audience will too. I look forward to enjoying your show tomorrow night." Hugh gave a bow over Delphina's hand and traipsed off to continue preparations, leaving sighing the moony-eyed adolescents and their smitten teacher to practice. Hugh didn't interfere with Delphina's coaching after observing her skills as she taught her first class.

"A bit smug there, my boy, aren't you?" Colonel Broadwater stood inside the door to the grounds, surrounded by newly set chairs. The audience would fill the observation deck, the lower deck, and a few more chairs fit between the benches down the length of the building.

Hugh clapped him on the shoulder. "I do believe she's coming around, sir."

"Considering the efforts you've put in to impress our lady teacher, I'd wonder if you've done anything else these last weeks." His laugh caused a rough catch in his throat.

"I assure you—"

"I know, son."

Hugh took the door as a fit of dry coughing struck the colonel. When it ended, he walked toward the hotel, matching the colonel's slower pace. His coughing had picked up by the day. The employees whispered concerns for their boss' health. Hugh stayed at the ready should he need to help as they entered the homey hotel lobby.

His voice a little hoarse, Colonel Broadwater asked, "Hugh, I think we're in need of a talk." He looked up the polished grand staircase. "Why don't you make sure I make it to my office and we can visit there over a cup of coffee?"

"I'm concerned for you, sir," Hugh admitted as he took his chair across the desk from the older man.

"Things are getting tougher for me." He coughed on and off through every sentence now. "I'm going to need to rely on you a bit more."

"Anything, Colonel. I hope you know I'll do anything I can to help."

"I'm not going to get better."

"Of course you are." Hugh leaned forward, putting his arms on the desk. "You're just in need of a rest. You take the time you need to recuperate and I'll watch out for your business in the meantime."

Broadwater took the spectacles off his nose, cleaned them, and replaced the lenses. "Listen to me, son." He reached out and put a hand on Hugh's forearm with all the pressure he could muster. "I need my affairs in order for the sake of not only my family, but all the families who need what the resort provides."

Hugh sucked air into collapsed lungs. "What do you need me to do, sir?"

"My last public event will be the water pageant

tomorrow night. After that, I'll turn over the management to you until I have a purchaser. Would you be agreeable to that?"

"Of course, sir. You can count on me."

"That, Hugh, I know. I'll be sure to suggest you stay on. In the best of circumstances, the new ownership would do well to keep all my staff. But, as you know, it's not something I can promise."

"But I can promise to see you and your family through until you no longer need me. I believe the same of the vast majority of your staff."

"Your Miss O'Connor?" Broadwater patted his arm and then leaned back, with his head on the chair. "What of her?"

"I think she'd be the first to stay."

"I'm asking what will become of your relationship with her?" The coughing took over again. "You're not required to tell me." His eyes softened. "I'm just an old man with a romantic bent." Another cough crackled under his handkerchief, now a constant companion that rarely made it back into his vest pocket. "I see a spark between you."

"I don't mind, sir. I'm planning to ask her to marry me."

"That little gal has no lack of choices in our fair city. I'd hate to see you miss out on the joy of a good wife."

"I'll take your advice to heart. But she has expressed the idea that she may not want to marry and have children."

His mentor stared at him in surprise. "Have you watched her with her students? Egads, son, have another talk with Miss O'Connor. Just don't wait too long or some other fellow might be having that talk for you." His energy expended, Charles Broadwater waved Hugh out of his office. "Another day for us. Go have that chat."

CHAPTER 11

EVERY LIGHT BLAZING to fill the aqua theatre, Delphina could feel the hum of anticipation for the water pageant buzzing through the throng. Her team of girls pranced around one another, feet constantly in motion, behind the giant waterfall. Now and again, one or another of the children would peek around the huge rock formation to wave at a mother or father.

Hugh's team of young men would end the evening with a full out race. But the way they started it would be quite exciting itself. Delphina would show an entire arena that women could not only be athletic, but they could create daredevil feats.

Walking to the shallow end, at the shorter one hundred-foot length, Hugh opened the extravaganza with a megaphone. "Ladies and gentlemen, welcome!" Polite applause echoed off the natatorium's walls and high ceiling. "With great pleasure, we present the Broadwater May Day Celebration featuring our own women's ornamental swimming team, the Helena Pipe and Drum Corps, and the men's competitive swimming team." More applause. "Without further ado, ladies take your places."

A line of adorable little girls marched out from behind the rocks formation to a smart drum cadence and lined the edge of the pool, hands in the classic opera pose. Delphina counted just loud enough for the girls to hear. "One, two, three!"

All at once, the line of miniature swimmers snapped their hands to their sides and took a step dropping into the pool with a half spin. They landed standing in their line facing the wall, laid arms across shoulders to connect everyone, and leaned back into a float as they kicked toward the central fountain.

The older girls performed the same entry move, then floated on their sides with arms raised and curved, mimicking a swan's neck. The cadence switched with them into a drumroll until they'd circled the little girls all around the fountain. Sliding arms down to clasp hands without disconnecting, the smaller girls kicked backward, letting go of hands when swimming under the bridges the older girls created as they stood and dove forward. The effect of a flower blooming continued as the girls of both circles traded places again. Then the little girls on the inner circle, both sets of swimmers twirled in opposite directions, arms reaching to the massive rafters high above, before the older girls kicked into a floating wheel that spun counter to the smaller wheel's clockwise turn.

As their kaleidoscope-style movements enthralled their audience, the women's team joined the designs. One-by-one, they linked together in another float, feet to shoulders, and created a large star pattern.

Quickly, as the audience watched the patterns in the

pool, Delphina climbed around and then inside the forty-foot boulder tower. The ladders, built inside for maintenance, gave her access to the top waterfall thirty feet above the plunge. She stepped out as the music built to a crescendo and the entire pool of swimmers framed the deep end, youngsters in the center of the arced line still able to stand in the shallow water with the women nearby protectively. Two of the older girls stood on plank diving boards, arms outstretched toward their teacher on the rock platform. The lights behind her, Delphina posed for a dramatic moment. As she swung her hands into position, the girls on the platform boards did the same. Synchronized, all the lower level divers performed a forward dive at the same time as the girls in the water ducked under the surface. As the four swam underwater, they came up with the rest of the team, feet pointed toward the center of the pool.

A quick glance and Delphina saw the men's team had taken their race positions at the far end of the pool. The girls splashed their feet in time with the band's music, creating an oval white cap around the entry point meant for their teacher's landing. The drumroll started again, but this time incorporating the bass drum as the signal for Delphina to lift off into a swan dive. A collective gasp of the crowd and she vaulted up first, and then tipping downward to the water below.

For a moment, the peace under the water enveloped her. Joy and air filled her lungs as she broke the surface and led the charge for the girls to swim as fast as they could to the side before the boys bore down on them. The energy in the aqua theatre was palpable. Moments later, the men's team finished their race to a roar of approval.

Delphina led both teams to line up along the sides of the plunge, facing out first, to take their bows. Every swimmer then swooped an arm to draw attention to the band at the far end of the auditorium. The Helena Pipe and Drum Corps, grown from the original eleven newsies two years ago to double the size, stood and also bowed to the audience.

The crowd rose to a standing ovation as the teams all turned to face the opposite side and bowed again. The joy emanating from every participant exploded into excited chatter.

Hugh quietly made his way, dripping from the swim, back to the top of the pool. Delphina joined him there. Taking her hand in his, he smiled. "And that, is entertainment." He winked before lifting the megaphone to his mouth. "We hope you enjoyed our first water pageant at the Hotel Broadwater and Natatorium. May there be many more." Thunderous applause met his announcement. Hugh had to wait several minutes to continue. "Our swimmers will join you in the hotel shortly. The dining rooms and salons are open for a reception where you can sign up for swimming instruction or one of the teams you enjoyed during tonight's extravaganza. We hope you'll continue to enjoy the extraordinary entertainment available at the Hotel Broadwater and Natatorium."

Children jumped out of line, searching for parents that still clapped and exclaimed their pride. Towels dropped over shoulders, quickly followed by adoring hugs.

Delphina let her gaze roam the huge mass of people. Every chair, two rows on each side of the pool and four rows deep in the observation deck, had been full. People crammed into nooks and crannies with standing room only.

Not one shocked gasp about the more modern swimming attire. Compliments and common requests for the costume pattern came instead. To her, that was the true success of the night.

As the area thinned of attendees, and they moved toward the reception, Mr. Broadwater and his wife walked a happy Wilder between them. The girl's face glowed pink from exertion still, but also exhilaration matching Delphina's feelings.

He didn't look well, but joy emanated from his entire being. "Well done, Miss O'Connor. I think you nearly gave me a heart attack with that high diving trick."

Lea brought a towel and wrapped her arms around Delphina's waist in a hug. "You were wonderful!"

Delphina hugged her back and then wrapped the towel around her shoulders. "You were too, Lea. I'm really proud of how fast you, and all the girls, learned that complex routine."

Julia Broadwater agreed, "It was pure magic, dear. I think you've done exactly what we expected of you."

After a few short coughs, Mr. Broadwater added his thoughts. "I couldn't be more pleased with the two of you. I expect the swimming classes to keep growing now." He took her hand. "Thank you."

Hugh put an arm around Delphina. "Sir, what do you say we hold a sign-up day for summer sports next week? We could feature all the outdoor activities like the horse-back trail rides, paddle-boats, and I was thinking of a croquet summer league."

"I think," Mr. Broadwater's wheezing stopped the conversation. He sucked in a rough breath. "I think you should go ahead. But now I need to rest." His eyes softened as he put a weak hand on Wilder's wet hair. "I'm grateful to have seen my daughter display such a beautiful talent." He looked back to Delphina. "Thank you. No matter how things go from here, I want you to know you are a very special young lady. Some young man is going to be very lucky," he paused and glanced at Hugh. "Yes, some young man will."

Did Hugh just turn red?

She smiled. "I appreciate such an honoring compliment, sir."

Mrs. Broadwater put her hand on her husband's back. "I think we need to get Wilder a bit of a treat and then it's time for us all to retire." The lady, ever gracious like her husband, supported him without drawing attention that he'd become the weaker vessel. "Don't you think so, dear?"

The love in his eyes had not dimmed for his still trim and youthful looking bride, though the last weeks took a toll on him. "Goodnight, you two. Such a well-done show."

As they walked down the exterior stairs and around the fountain of a boy holding a boot, she wrapped an arm around her husband. Wilder burst past Hugh and Delphina and caught up with her parents, wet hair stringing down the back of her school dress.

Delphina watched them as the doors closed. "If that kind of family weren't so rare, I might be swayed."

"What if someone cared about you enough to want that kind of family?" Hugh asked.

She stepped back from the door as another group of people congratulated them on the program as they left.

Once alone again, she tried to convince him of the futility. "Really, Hugh, I was being kind. I find it hard to believe it possible." Delphina's eyes clouded. "What an amazing man."

Pointing out at the retreating family through the glass inset, Hugh said, "It's right in front of you. That kind of family exists."

"But I said it's rare."

"Why? Why do you think it's so rare?"

"Don't you hear the married couples around you? They're so busy, so focused on everything but each other and their children." She shook her head, "No. I don't want that kind of life." Delphina chose to meet his eyes straight on. "If you believe in fairy tale love, I can show you girls getting off the train one day and getting married the next, right here in Helena. I can show you women who have dreams one day and the next she's left them behind to support her husband's. How many couples have a marriage that lets both people grow into their potential?"

"And I can show you more couples like the Broadwaters, the Shanahans, the Russells and my own parents. How many would you like me to name before you believe happy marriages with mutual respect and support are possible?"

"I–" With examples like those, what kind of proof did she need?

CHAPTER 12

HUGH HELD a black umbrella above them as he climbed the hill beside Delphina. The press of people and carriages filled the grounds. Four special trains arrived, one after another, for Colonel Broadwater's funeral. The viewing procession would take all day with the thousands of friends coming to support the family. As he spread a wool blanket in new spring grass, even the hillside began to fill with the overflow of mourners, despite the colder day and bit of snow still melting from a late, but not unheard of, storm.

"This should keep us dry and comfortable." He offered a hand to seat Delphina. "I thought you could do with a short time away from grounds, but..." Huge spread a hand, gesturing at the pockets of people already following their example.

She spread her black dress off to the side, making room for Hugh to join her. "At least we can breathe up here." Delphina's voice quivered as she perused the grounds spread out like a postcard not far below. "He's never going to see his dream succeed."

"Yes, yes, he did. He built this amazing place."

"But it never operated at a profit. There are more people in that procession than ever graced the plunge in all the time it's been open." The line backed up the road into the forty-acre property. "He never felt the satisfaction of knowing his dream would succeed."

"Delphina, I don't think that's the point at all. We see things as a success or a failure if they make money or fame. But that's not how God works. He works on an eternal level."

Her black bonnet brim blocked the late morning sun as it lifted to warm the day. "You know what I meant." Her eyes dulled when she turned to look at him. "If a man can affect a state and so many lives the way Charles Broadwater did, then why couldn't he see his own vision come to fruition?"

"How do you know the Hotel Broadwater and Natatorium wasn't successful? He built an amazing resort. But look at all the families he supported through the jobs, all the people whose lives were positively affected because one man had a dream in the first place."

Delphina delayed a response as she considered Hugh's profound thoughts. She watched the carriages and mourners draped in black creep forward. "But wouldn't you want to know? Don't you think he felt depressed in the end?"

"Did you see his face from the family suite in the balcony? He loved the spectacle of the people. He watched families play croquet, sit in the swings, and just stroll the grounds. I think he experienced elation each time anyone enjoyed the specialness he built.

Hugh touched her cheek and gently turned her face

toward his. "I see the lives he touched through his lifetime. Look at the fact that he brought you out here to work. It changed your life, didn't it? I know he changed mine. I had the honor of mentoring under his tutelage for four years. Now I wonder whom I'll be able to mentor. Whose life will I influence? How many families can I support through the business ventures still ahead of me because one man poured trust and wisdom into me?"

"You're right. I hadn't thought of it that way. Some of the biggest opportunities in the world started as a dream."

"It isn't how rich we become. It's how we've enriched the lives around us. That's what I learned from Colonel Broadwater, to be a man that helps others to succeed—then when I close my eyes for the last time, I'll be content with how I lived. He brought a lot of joy into the lives around him. I hope someone will be able to say the same about me. Can you imagine what's happening in heaven right now?"

"In heaven?"

"I see the Lord greeting our friend. I see him showing one short, bald man how the world changed because he was a servant, obedient, and willing to act on the dreams he'd been given. Because of that courage, Charles A. Broadwater inspired thousands of people and helped Montana become a state. His life was a success. He didn't need a building to prove it or this long line of well-wishers."

Delphina smiled. "I want to be the kind of a woman that influences others to dream as big as they can. I want to bring joy to those around me, too."

"If we continued to act as a team, I think we can both do that and more."

She looked at Hugh, but hesitated. "Both dreams?"

"I want you to have dreams and to get them. Delphina, that is what God gave you. I'd have a lot to answer for if I derailed your God-given purpose." His eyes crinkled into a loving smile. "The day I stand before his throne, the last thing I want to hear is the Lord asking me why I would stand in his way."

She gazed up from under her bonnet with such a beautiful, soft countenance. "I think Mr. Broadwater will hear that the Lord is pleased with the way he inspired us to embrace and reach for our goals."

"Wherever we go from here, Delphina O'Connor, I'd like it to be together." He cupped her cheek.

There wasn't any surprise as she tipped her face into his palm. Instead, her eyes swept closed. He felt the tickle of long black lashes trace against the warmth of his thumb. A thrill washed over Hugh as she said, "Me too."

Hugh wrapped an arm around her. "Would you be willing to take the plunge and marry me?"

"As long as you don't keep me in the shallow end."

A quick burst of wind ruffled, blew Hugh's hat off into Delphina's lap. "Never." He reached for it at the same time as she did. "We're a team. Helpmeets to one another." He met her eyes and then his gaze dropped to her mouth, longing to touch his lips to hers.

"Then where you go, I will go." She smoothed his hair back into place and traced her fingertips back to his neck. The intimate touch drew him toward her.

Hugh lowered the umbrella, blocking any onlookers but those in heaven, and kissed Delphina's upturned lips.

READ A SAMPLE OF THE NEXT BOOK...

FLOWER OF THE ROCKIES — BOOK 4

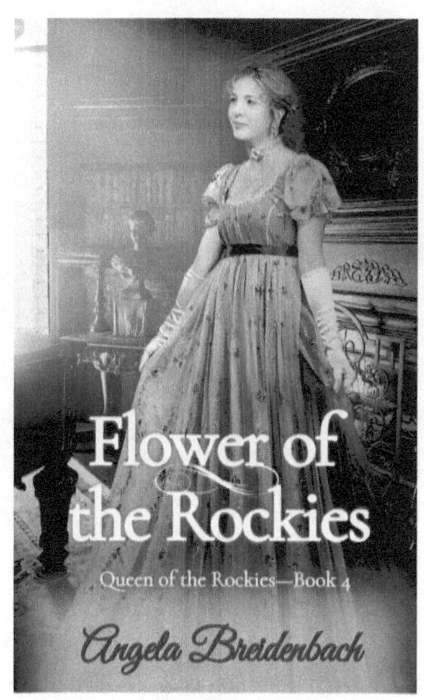

FLOWER OF THE ROCKIES

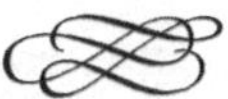

CHAPTER 1

June, 1894

Infamous. She couldn't walk down a street in town without drawing attention—even fully clothed. No matter that she wore widow's garb for a year. Longer than most in a town where men outnumbered women since its inception. No matter that she never looked at a man, other than her husband in two years. The men knew who she was and they stared. Therefore, the women knew and they ostracized. But they didn't know she'd just been fleeced by a scoundrel! Would they care if they did?

Emmalee Warren seethed as the layered ruffles of her cotton skirt swished around her white kid boots like the summer windstorms blowing through the passes. Woe to another man that ever crossed her path! Only one had ever been kind. Unfortunately, every gold-digger within a day's ride wanted to stake a claim on her, since Charles died in the cave in. Silver mines meant nothing these days. But owning a gold mine… if her past occupation hadn't already marked her, being the heiress to a working gold mine brought men out like ants to a sugar pile. She didn't need any of the pests. What she did need, right now, was a good lawyer!

The grocer's shop door opened, spilling a youngster and his mama into her path. The woman's smile flared as she made eye contact.

Emmalee smiled back.

"Oh!" And as fleeting, the good woman's smile faltered. "Quickly son, move quickly." Her words not even whispered as she snagged his hand and tugged the boy away.

Emmalee masked her disappointment under the wide brim of the elegant rose covered hat. It'd been the first smile she'd seen in a long time. "Excuse me." She moved aside, allowing the mother and child to pass onto the sidewalk. Emmalee would not lower herself to treat another poorly. But after attempting for two years to be courteous to respectable folks, what more could she do? No one knew her or bothered, unless they wanted something. No one cared that she wanted a fresh start. That she didn't want to go back from whence she came.

The woman covered the little boy's eyes. "We don't notice people like that, Erwin."

"Why Mama? She's pretty. Why don't we notice people like that?"

"Shh, don't be rude, son."

People like that. Emmalee blinked back a sharp sting behind her eyelids. First it had been her body, and now the money and mine her husband left behind. On such a sunny day, the scent of green grass in the breeze off the mountains, her heart suffered a drought near as bad as the Great Plains experienced these last few years. What was it yesterday's unexpected caller had said as he'd offered the last in a long line of inappropriate proposals?

"I shore liked the way that lacy dress fit them there bosoms."

She shuddered. Chicago Joe's Coliseum Theatre promoted that distinctive fashion statement, an all lace dressing gown that clung to her curvaceous figure. Men flocked to see her. She forced the memory away.

Emmalee glanced over her shoulder with a pang in her empty womb. What would she have said in the other woman's place? The mother kept a hand on the boy's neck, making it impossible for him to sneak a peek at a woman who didn't deserve to be seen. The cowlick in his brown hair popped between his mother's gloved fingers.

No, that kind of behavior wouldn't have been a Warren family value. But then Charles Warren's mother had also been a lady of a certain profession. He'd been sent to the best schools she could afford. He didn't share a distaste of those less fortunate. A fond smile crossed Emmalee's lips. She missed the way he'd read the newspaper to her after dinner. Without him, she floated in a disconnected life, not fitting in anywhere anymore.

Twenty-five. A little too late to wish for a child that wouldn't be in Emmalee's future. With no husband, and the doctor's report, well, she couldn't wallow there now. She needed a lawyer, not a ridiculous pretense she'd ever have a family that people like her didn't deserve.

A one-year marriage couldn't create respectability or a baby for her husband. Not after being a well-known soiled dove for the most famous madam in Montana, Chicago Joe

—the woman Emmalee couldn't forgive. Josephine had the blessing of owning property and had somehow finagled her way into respectability in Helena's society—that is until the 1885 ordinance pushed them all into the shadows. If the silver crash hadn't happened last July, Emmalee might have never been let go from her lease. But Charles struck gold instead of silver. He offered cash for his favorite dalliance in the last bordello left to Chicago Joe. Cash the madam badly needed to settle debts. Cash that freed one popular Miss Emmie, Darling of the West, from an occupation that awarded a lone girl survival in the unforgiving frontier, albeit also the expectation of a shorter lifespan.

Banking would be much easier if she'd been allowed to get more than a third-grade education. As would reading thick contracts, like the one stuffed in the envelope inside her reticule with the bank statement showing a measly hundred dollars instead of a thousand. How could she know the partner Charles trusted meant to fleece her? How did Chicago Joe succeed when she couldn't read or write either? But then that was the argument—education. Who needed a seductress that could read and write? Her job skills were more of the… physical nature. Scratching a name was more than enough in her profession. Too bad Miss Emmie couldn't even do that right!

A cowboy hooked a double take from his saddle, then reined his gelding into a fast redirection. The roan stamped his front hooves and squealed displeasure before settling into obedience. "Ho there, little lady!" He reined away from a carriage and came back for another pass. "Miss Ellie, I heard you was available agin."

She ignored him, walking on. Ellie, for pity's sake. At least he could have gotten her name right!

"I jes wanna talk." He called from nearly the middle of the street.

Picking up her pace, Emmalee averted her eyes and pressed her lips together at his transparent persistence. She refused to acknowledge the commotion he'd created or the stares from anyone, man or woman. She also refused to be caught in yet another annoying conversation professing undying love from a no-good money-grubber. Even an uneducated woman knew enough to avoid a lout drawing unwanted attention on the street. She switched her parasol into the other hand, blocking the annoyance from view.

Although some of the men pressing for her affections may have been customers, they were still unwelcome. Miss Emmie had quit that life. To lock away the past, she'd need to sell her home and move away—start over where no one knew Miss Emmie. The padlock on the iron cage around her heart could only be accessed from the inside—the key conveniently buried deep. She'd certainly learned that while under Chicago Joe's tutelage. And she refused to go back. But if her bank account didn't have the funds, thanks to a dishonest mining partner, what would she do to survive?

Emmalee closed her parasol and grasped the door handle of the Goodkind building. She lifted her chin. Survive she would! But not if she stayed in Helena, MT.

CHAPTER 2

RICHARD LEWIS SET down the paperwork. "Madam—"

"Don't call me that." Her eyes flashed. "Don't ever call me that again."

"I meant no disrespect, Mrs. Warren."

"Didn't you?"

He hadn't meant to insinuate age. "No, I truly didn't. I wouldn't insult a lady on purpose." It'd be foolish to alienate any client during the economically uncertain times. Lesson one, with this client. Watch his words.

She gave him a direct stare. "All right, then Mrs. Warren is fine." She nodded to the documents on his desk. A tinge of desperation laced her words. "Will you be able to take my case?"

"Yes. I've only skimmed the pages, but I think you have a good chance of proving criminal behavior in court, Mrs. Warren, if we can prove he intended to commit fraud." For the sake of clear communication, Richard asked, "Are there any other words I might offend you with?"

"Are you having sport with me?" She stood and extended her hand to take back the paperwork.

Richard's brow wrinkled. "Sport? Why would I—"

She sized him up a moment, then sat back down. "You mean to say you aren't aware of who I am?"

Besides a very lovely lady with a very touchy vocabulary? "Mrs. Warren, have we met before? It's not a large city, and I haven't been here long, but I don't remember crossing paths with you or your husband."

"No, but most folks know of me."

Know what? He shook his head. She could be the Queen of Sheba as far as he knew. She was definitely as mysterious.

"When did you arrive then?" Mrs. Warren folded her arms and waited.

"I came last June, right before the silver was devalued." This appointment was not going well at a time he really needed new clientele. Quite a few businesses closed their doors and moved on. "I'm sorry to offend you again, ma'am, but I have no idea."

The small upturn on the corner of her mouth fascinated him. But she said nothing. What would she look like with the glow of a full, sunny smile? He tapped the pile between them. "This will wasn't drawn up by my predecessor or myself." Buying a small legal firm might not have been the wisest investment in hindsight. But he had to start somewhere.

"That firm closed their doors and moved to Butte last year along with the accountant." She shook her head. "I've had to rely on Charles' business partner, Mr. Steven Brown, until now."

"Ah, that explains why you sought out new representation." He folded his hands on top of the desk. "Why did you trust him?"

"I had no reason to distrust him. My husband and he had been partners for several years."

"Why do you think this Steven Brown took advantage of you?"

She searched his face. "You might as well hear it from me first if you're going to represent me." Her features stiffened, as did her back. "I met my husband while working at The Coliseum Theatre." She gave him that direct look again, as if she challenged him.

Richard kept his voice as level as possible. "I see." A bordello. She appeared so proper, a young widow who had only recently come out of mourning. But the brunette beauty in the chair across from him had been a—

"Give me my papers please."

"Are you firing me before we start?" Lesson two. No extended pauses, shocked or not. This lady could read people well.

"You're willing to help me?"

"Of course." Richard tipped his head. How to say it? "You've been wronged, Mrs. Warren. If you'll let me, I intend to do my best efforts to right that wrong."

She pursed her lips and looked out the open window behind him while deciding. Those big brown eyes filled with luminous light, as if God hung a star in each. "All right then."

He swallowed to bring his mind back to the subject. "Mrs. Warren, tell me how you discovered this contract was incorrect to your agreement?"

"I attempted to draw funds to pay my bills this morning." She swallowed. "The clerk warned me my funds were getting low. My husband's partner had withdrawn a substantial sum without my knowledge."

"He's on your account?"

"Yes. According to the clerk, I gave him access with this contract last month. But Mr. Brown's ability to withdraw funds was never discussed, nor would I have done that."

Richard licked a finger and thumbed through the many pages until he found a small sentence granting access to the bank account. "Mrs. Warren, what did you think this contract meant?"

"I thought it gave permission to my husband's partner to work my half of the mine and to hire men for me. He was to act as a foreman, then deposit gold from the mine into the account."

Richard nodded as he checked her interpretation with the document. "So you didn't read this line?" He turned the page around and pointed at the center of page nine.

"Never did we discuss Mr. Brown's ability to withdraw from my account."

"But it's here. You didn't see it?"

She breathed in slowly as she directed her attention to the words. Then, slowly, she raised her gaze to meet his. "No."

He flipped a few pages back in the packet. "I don't see where you signed." He slid the pages apart. The only thing on the last page was a poorly formed capital "E".

"I made my mark."

Richard's head snapped up from the document. "Please don't be offended, but I need to ask if you know how to read and write?"

With a tight expression, she switched her gloves into her left hand. "No, Mr. Lewis, I do not. If you must know, I never passed the third grade." Her hands fidgeted with the fingers on the gloves. "But I am working on it. Teaching oneself reading and writing is not the easiest thing to do."

He nodded. A protective instinct rose within Richard. "Then I'll be sure to read anything you need out loud and answer any questions you have. I want you to understand everything and base your decisions on full knowledge."

"I would appreciate that." She sat back in the chair. "Go ahead. I have time."

"I hadn't planned—"

She raised a brow.

Rule three—expect the unexpected. Clearly, Mrs. Warren meant to hear all ten pages now. His next appointment wasn't for a few hours yet, since clients were dwindling. Why not? "I'll order some coffee and rolls, then we'll start." He put a note in the dumbwaiter.

A short time later, the grocer's wife responded by sending up a pot. They had an arrangement. The grocer carried a monthly tab. Coffee could be ordered, added to the tab, and Mrs. Bach would deliver it for an extra penny per request via the dumbwaiter. Well worth avoiding three stories of stairs balancing a tray of slippery dishes—or for clients that stayed through lunch.

Richard finished reading the last page. He sorted them back into consecutive order and tapped them on the desk to straighten the stack. "I'll need a few days to research with the bank and the county clerk. Would that be acceptable?"

"Yes." As she stood, she held out a hand. "Thank you, both for reading the contract to me and for coffee." Then she gifted him with a genuine smile that reached those big, brown eyes.

Eyes that intrigued him. He stood, mesmerized, and took her soft hand in his. Her handshake wasn't regal or limp or rough. She made her agreement with confidence, though she didn't allow the touch to linger.

"Mrs. Warren, everyone deserves for their rights to be protected. I intend to stop your account from being plundered."

She seemed more relaxed than when she'd arrived, almost at ease. "When should we meet again?"

"This time next week? That will give me time to research the claim filing and bank policies."

"Yes, I'll look forward to what you find out."

He saw her to the door. Would he earn another smile when they next met?

I love Montana. You, dear reader, may have figured that out already. Sharing special spots and experiences is pure joy. Do you love discovering secret corners in the world to treasure? Come visit a few precious treasures in Montana and create some amazing memories of beauty, relaxation, and country pace of life. Keep reading for my *Top 3 Montana Hot Springs*.

Though the Broadwater Hotel and Natatorium our heroine, Delphina, discovered in Helena no longer exists, you'll see another of the same name on the site I share a little later in this travel tips article. The new one is a popular fitness club, just not the original.

But lucky us, Montana is still dotted generously with natural hot springs. Some are a hike into the mountains while others have been modernized into a series of public swimming pools. Plunge in and soak your stress away!

Let me share a few of my favorites with you and tell you why. Then check the links I'm including to see for yourself.

Please remember this is a book written on a specific date and those links can change over time. If they have, I've done my best to share the correct link as I write this for you in the Fall of 2021.

1. Bozeman Hot Springs — 12 pools. Uh huh, 12! Our family has had fabulous memories here in the upscale, modern facility. No hotel, but there are lovely places to stay in and around Bozeman. This special spot is a little pricier than others, but well worth it. The concerts on the pool deck and colorful lights in vibrant purples, reds, blues, pinks, and more go with the music. The mists lift off the water making the ambience mystical and mysterious, especially at night. Fitness options exist because it's also a fitness center. Skiing is fairly close and Bozeman is a main airport even though the city itself is not a large one. The surrounding area is stunning in all seasons. But seriously, concerts on the pool deck outside! Mood lighting! Mystical mists!

    https://bozemanhotsprings.co

2. Fairmont Hot Springs — There are several pools that range in depth and temperature. They're indoor and out like the Bozeman Hot Springs. They'll even sell pool toys and floats for little ones. The long, curly waterslide happens to be a family favorite for us! The indoor-accessed slide spins riders round and round until they land in a deep outdoor pool. But be advised each use of the slide has a fee or you can get a wrist band. There's a restaurant, hotel, and campground. We've stayed at both the hotel and the campground — which is an easy walk to the pools and has a playground for munchkins. The facilities are a little worn, but based on the busy clientele, nobody really cares. Just be prepared that it won't look like a five-star though you'll find a wonderful spa. Yes, I have tried the spa and loved my massage. Hubby and I had an amazing romantic weekend away. Okay, I went to the spa while he had to go to a business meeting. Nope. I don't feel badly about that at all. Fairmont is very family-friendly and constantly trying to improve their facilities. We've been to Fairmont, only 90 minutes from Missoula, many times over the years with children and now grandchildren. We've gone for business, family, and a couples get-away. You'll have a great time and wonderful memories.

https://www.fairmontmontana.com

3. Jackson Hot Springs — Relaxing and rustic time travel experience! We took our family for a true Christmas get-away. We wanted to get away from technology, rushing, and commercialization. With six kids, owning a business, managing extended family needs, and my writing/speaking, we needed to literally unplug everyone from the crazy pace. We had the best family vacation with a long Christmas weekend! There's no TV in the rooms, but they're very comfortable. The log cabins come in various sleeping options. We went swimming in the reasonable, but smaller-sized hot spring pool and loved it. In the lodge, the restaurant/bar had everything we needed including a fantastic shuffle board game we all created family tournaments around. Then we spent a day snowmobiling around the area. Rustic, yes. Uncomfortable, no. The experience is down-to-earth and exceptional. Remember to prepare the kiddos that they aren't going to spend all their time watching a screen. This is true Montana immersion they'll never forget if you all get out into the real world and off the virtual world. If you need to unplug and breathe like we did, Jackson Hot Springs is your spot. Do call ahead and ask about the facility, any cold weather expectations, and any allergy or other needs. We found them very accomodating which made our stay all the better. Visit their website:

https://jacksonhotspringslodge.com

Yes, there are a ton of hot springs here in the Treasure State that range from small pond-like holes in the mountains to super state-of-the-art modern swimming pools. I shared my top three. We've chosen them for different reasons at different stages of our family life. You might have different criteria than I do. When you come visit, there's great advice on the experience you and your family want by checking the Visit Montana website: www. visitmt.com or check the specific page with a helpful map:

https://www.visitmt.com/things-to-do/shopping-and-leisure/hot-springs-resorts-and-pools

Come any season. Remember a winter snowmobiling, snowshoeing, skiing, dunk in the hot springs is as amazing as summer hiking, fishing, camping, and dunking in the hot springs. Regardless of what season you visit Montana, she is the secret treasure in the United States. Shh… don't tell my secret ;)

I hope you found this little travel tips article helpful. Each book in the Queen of the Rockies series has a unique travel tips article for you to collect. By the time we're done with all six books, you'll have your own travel guide!

—Angela

I hope you enjoyed book 3, *Heart of the Rockies*, in the Queen of the Rockies series. I loved sharing a little true Montana history about our Hotel Broadwater and Natatorium through Delphina's and Hugh's love story, and also introducing the beginnings of my favorite sport, synchronized swimming in its infancy.

Sadly, the resort was demolished after a devastating 1935 earthquake and a series of events too much for the grand lady. She just couldn't recover. Where she stood, private land exists. But the hot springs does, too.

As I mentioned at the beginning, the 1890s in Montana could easily be compared to the legend of Camelot. "For happily ever-aftering is here in Camelot…" Yes, the mists have swallowed up some of our most incredible history, but we won't let it be forgotten. I wrote other stories that tell what happens as Montana becomes a state in the Queen of the Rockies series. I hope you'll help me preserve the memories of the people and places by reading these books, then telling others about them. Don't forget to tell your own family history stories in the process. Your stories are important to preserve, too.

Finally, I need to ask a favor. Reviews help books sell. Would you kindly leave a review on your favorite site such Bookbub.com, as ChristianBook.com, Litsy, Goodreads, Amazon, or any other review site? Your feedback is important to me! Reviews can be hard to come by these days. You, the reader, have the power now to make or break a book.

Pop over to my website to see what's happening in books, speaking, travel, and genealogy. I have a newsletter that goes out with new releases, genealogy tips, and another one that features my fe-lion personal assistant now and then.

Thank you so much for reading *Heart of the Rockies*, spending time with the historic people of Helena, and I hope you'll also enjoy my other books in the Queen of the Rockies series. But most of all, thank you for spending time with me. I'll see you shortly in 1894, with the next book in this series, Flower of the Rockies.

You can write to me at: angela@angelabreidenbach.-com, I do answer emails personally. It's really fun to hear from readers, often very encouraging. Please visit me at: AngelaBreidenbach.com.

Appreciatively,
Angela Breidenbach

Did you miss the beginning of the Queen of the Rockies series?

What if you were caught doing something good, but the man you loved didn't see it that way? Meet Calista Blythe and Albert Shanahan in 1889…

Queen of the Rockies (Queen of the Rockies, Book 1) by Angela Breidenbach ~ 1889 (Helena, MT): *What will her courage cost?* As Montana emerges into statehood, one woman must decide if social pressure will prevail when she hides an endangered child, risking her own future happiness. Queen of the Rockies — Book 1 of 6, opens this delightful series of Gilded Age historical romances peppered with genealogical tidbits.

Song of the Rockies, Book 2, 1890 Montana historical.

Song of the Rockies is the story of a sweet music teacher and eleven boys given one chance or else! Evan Russell lost everything—his ranch, his wife, and now, after trusting relatives with his young son, even the little boy is missing. How can a beautiful symphony of the heart come from such chaos?

Mirielle Sheehan, a music teacher at an exclusive boys' school, believes scholarships for disadvantaged boys will solve the plight of hopeless homeless children. Mirielle's challenge is to turn eleven street ruffians of various ages into stellar, disciplined boys with a future. Most think guttersnipes like this should be sold into indenture to learn a trade or pressed into the military. Get those miscreants off the streets!

Evan Russell, new mining millionaire, lost everything in the disastrous winter of 1886. Then his wife died leaving him with a son. Relatives in Helena offer a safe home for the child while Evan must find work in the mines. When he returns, he's devastated to learn the entire family perished in a fire, and his son has never been found. Though he gained a fortune, he's lost everything he valued!

Romantic, sweet adventure set in picturesque Helena, Montana written by a bestselling author who is also a professional genealogist.

Thank you for reading the first two chapters of Flower of the Rockies. Please visit your favorite store or Angela's website to get your copy and read the rest. Watch for the rest of the books in this series by signing up for my new releases via Bookbub or my newsletter.

BOOKS BY ANGELA BREIDENBACH

Romantic Fiction:

(Contemporary)

A Healing Heart

(Historical)

Queen of the Rockies, Queen of the Rockies book 1

Song of the Rockies, Queen of the Rockies book 2

Heart of the Rockies, Queen of the Rockies book 3

Flower of the Rockies, Queen of the Rockies book 4

Bride of the Rockies, Queen of the Rockies book 5

Flame of the Rockies, Queen of the Rockies book 6

Mail-Order Bride Standoff (Barbour Publishing)

Non-fiction:

Gems of Wisdom: The Treasure of Experience

(2nd edition reprint)

For other titles by Angela, please visit AngelaBreidenbach.com

ABOUT THE AUTHOR

Angela Breidenbach is a bestselling Montana author, professional genealogist, and speaker. As a Montana author it's one of her favorite places to write about, whether in an historical or contemporary setting. She lives in Montana with her hubby and Muse, a trained fe-lion, who shakes hands, rolls over, and jumps through a hoop. Surprisingly, Angela can also.

Catch her show and podcast, Genealogy Publishing Coach! You'll find it on her website, Youtube, and your favorite podcast app.

https://AngelaBreidenbach.com
Bookbub/Facebook/Twitter/Pinterest/Instagram:
@AngBreidenbach

facebook.com/AngBreidenba

twitter.com/AngBreidenbach

instagram.com/AngBreidenbach

bookbub.com/authors/AngBreidenbach

goodreads.com/Angela_Breidenbach

youtube.com/AngelaBreidenbach

amazon.com/Angela-Breidenbach/e/B00460W4F4

pinterest.com/AngBreidenbach

www.ingramcontent.com/pod-product-compliance
Lightning Source LLC
Chambersburg PA
CBHW030100130726
47902CB00018B/2062